ERLE STANLEY GARDNER

THE DA
BREAKS A SEAL

HOUSE OF
STRATUS

This edition published in 2000 by House of Stratus, an imprint of Stratus Holdings plc, 24c Old Burlington Street, London, W1X 1RL, UK.

www.houseofstratus.com

Typeset, printed and bound by House of Stratus.

A catalogue record for this book is available from the British Library.

ISBN 1-84232-098-X

CAST OF CHARACTERS

MAJOR DOUG SELBY
Ex-DA of Madison County, spends his five-day furlough matching wits with a murderer.

HATTIE IRWIN
Little woman from Kansas, awarded first place in a contest she never heard about.

SYLVIA MARTIN
Reporter for the *Clarion*, has her own ideas about tracking the facts.

A B CARR
Criminal lawyer with a facile tongue and a million-dollar client.

REX BRANDON
Sheriff of the tough and true school, with all of the work and none of the laurels.

CARL GIFFORD
District attorney, bent on political plums and pettiness.

INEZ STAPLETON
Attractive counsellor-at-law, whose client's case takes a turn towards murder.

CAST OF CHARACTERS

FRANK NORWALK
Proprietor of Madison Hotel, finds a guest who checked out as a corpse.

FRED ALBION ROFF
Ordered two breakfasts before he died.

OTTO LARKIN
Chief of police, whose bluster is exceeded only by his boners.

ANITA ELDON
Beauteous blonde from Hollywood, comes to town to be made an heiress.

HARRY PERKINS
The coroner with a happy outlook.

ELEANOR PRESTON
May have made her will under undue influence.

HERVEY PRESTON
Surviving brother of Eleanor Preston.

MARTHA OTLEY
Eleanor Preston's housekeeper and companion.

HENRY FARLEY
Hotel waiter, the 'cup bearer'.

COLEMAN DEXTER
Prospective fruit grove buyer, saw a woman leave the murdered man's room.

DOC THURMAN
Physician on the case.

W BARCLAY STANTON
Small-town lawyer with an unstaunched flow of rhetoric, counsel for Hervey Preston.

BARBARA HONCUTT
Inez Stapleton's client, cut out of a million-dollar will.

CARL HASTLE
Comes to town in a rumpled suit with a white gardenia.

ELMER D FLORIS
The man in charge of bookings.

MRS DIXON
Former employee of the late Eleanor Preston.

FRANKLIN L DAWSON
Witness at the signing of Eleanor Preston's will.

HELEN ELIZABETH CORNING
Sister of Martha Otley, and A B Carr's star witness.

CHAPTER ONE

The transcontinental Pullmans, creaking like some huge snake whose vertebrae had gone dry, crawled across the last weary miles of desert. Joshua palms, thrusting up grotesque spine-covered arms, made the scenery resemble some fantastic reconstruction of life on another planet. Yet within forty minutes the train would wind its way through a canyon and shortly thereafter glide through the dark green of fertile orange groves.

Doug Selby, distinguished looking in his major's uniform, and with five days of his furlough still to run, let his eyes drink in the familiar scenery. The train topped a summit, and Selby knew that he was once more in Madison County, where for years he had been the district attorney. Rex Brandon, the grizzled ex-cowboy who had been elected sheriff at the same bitterly contested election, had gone into the courthouse with him, and the pair had stayed in there, fighting an organized opposition, until that fateful December seventh when a bigger, more desperate fight had called Doug Selby into the Army.

The train was gathering speed now, twisting and turning down sharp grades. Another few minutes would see them in Madison City, and Selby looked up at the porter who stood beside him with brush and shoe cloth.

'Yes, suh. Little brush, suh?'

Selby followed the porter into the vestibule, where a dollar bill brought white teeth into smiling prominence. Returning to his seat, Selby noticed that the porter was bending over a seat farther up the aisle. 'Yes, Ma'am. Like to be brushed, please, Ma'am? Next stop is Madison City.'

Selby had heretofore given this passenger only casual attention. She was a work-worn, vague little woman with dark, tired eyes that had been pulled far back into their sockets. She was probably in the sixties, and would weigh little more than a hundred pounds; yet she asked no favours of anyone. Her motions were swift and sure, and she kept her back straight, her chin up. Apparently, however, somewhere in her work-worn life she had forgotten how to smile. There was about her the aftermath of a great weariness as though she had toiled through more than her share of hard work and wanted rest now that it was too late to relax.

She followed the porter demurely, was brushed off, and handed him a tip which had been tightly held in escrow in her closed palm, a tip which the porter transferred to his pocket without the slightest change in the impersonal courtesy of his expression.

Selby watched the woman return to her seat.

A dining car waiter entered the car, walked directly to the spry little woman. He was carrying a white pasteboard box.

'Here yuah is, Ma'am. Been keeping it in the icebox. All nice and fresh, I hope.'

Once more the gloved hand passed out a tip, this time after dipping frugally into the purse.

'Yes, Ma'am. Thank you kindly, Ma'am.'

The dining car waiter looked at the tip, glanced at the Pullman car porter. Both men grinned.

Selby found himself idly wondering about the contents of the white pasteboard box, watched the woman bustling about with prim, last-minute preparations for leaving the train. He saw the porter come for her bags, help her on with her coat, and then, as the porter picked up Selby's bags, Selby saw the woman open the pasteboard box.

It contained three gardenias made into an attractive corsage. The bony fingers moved with swift dexterity, pinning the corsage to the lapel of her coat.

The ex-district attorney decided to keep an eye on this poker-faced little woman who had so carefully secured for herself a gardenia corsage somewhere in the Middle West and had it kept on ice all the way to Southern California. It would be interesting to see just what type of man was responsible for this romantic gesture on the part of a woman who seemed so utterly self-contained.

The train debouched from the walled canyon. Almost at once the deep green of the orange orchards furnished a welcome relief to eyes that had accustomed themselves to the pastel shades of the desert, and the eye-aching glare of pitiless sunlight.

The train rumbled across a bridge and Selby glimpsed the white houses and red-tiled roofs of Madison City. His eyes softened with memories. Every bit of this country held history for him. There had been a body found under this trestle; that case up there on Orange Grove Heights had been one of the most puzzling murder cases in Southern California; and in that massive white courthouse Selby had worked, fought, and ...

The train slowed to a creaking stop. The porter opened the vestibule, handed down the baggage, then helped the woman who was wearing the white gardenias to alight. A moment later, Selby was on the station platform, looking around at old familiar scenes.

Nearly a dozen people had left the train at Madison City, and Selby saw Sylvia Martin, reporter for the *Clarion*, moving about looking the crowd over. Then her eyes swung toward the rear of the train. She caught sight of Selby, and suddenly ceased all motion, standing incredulously silent in the midst of the bustling train-time activity. Then she was running.

'*Doug!* Doug Selby!' she cried.

Selby met her halfway.

'What on earth brings you here?'

Selby looked down into eager eyes and a flushed face. 'I've been transferred to some destination out of San Francisco, and have five days left of a seven-day furlough. I decided to spend it here.'

'Why, Doug, you old meanie! Why *didn't* you let me know?'

'Well, I got here as soon as a letter would, and it seemed rather foolish to write. What are you doing down here? Has the town got so small you're forced to cover the trains now?'

She said laughingly, 'I came down because old A B C did, and almost anything he does is news.'

'Good old A B C,' Selby replied laughingly. 'I'd been wondering about him. Is he still the same human enigma?'

'Just the same as ever. He still claims he came here to retire from his city law practice. He still contends as gravely as ever that he's annoyed to find his former clients won't let him take life easy ... There he is now. Looks as though he didn't find the party he expected to meet.'

Selby glanced over the heads of the crowd to study the placid strength of A B Carr's features. A skilled courtroom dramatist, the big city criminal lawyer, known affectionately to the underworld as old A B C, managed to invest his every move with the dignity of a Shakespearean actor.

'He's looking for someone,' Sylvia said. 'Heavens, Doug, he didn't know *you* were coming?'

Selby laughed. 'Of course not. If anyone had known it, you'd have been the one. If Carr doesn't lead you to a story, Sylvia, I'll give you a lead on a swell human interest yarn.'

'What is it? I'm all ears.'

'See that little woman over there with the dark coat and a gardenia corsage?'

'Yes.'

'She's a sweet little old thing coming to Madison City on a mission of romance. The white gardenia corsage was carefully preserved all the way from somewhere around Kansas just so she could be all fresh and attractive – or else to enable the masculine part of the romantic alliance to identify her. Bet she'd give you a nice story if you interviewed her.'

Sylvia Martin studied the woman. 'She's learned to be self-sufficient and self-contained, Doug. She'd tell me to mind my own business. Let's watch to see who the man is ... Doug! *She's* the one A B C is meeting. And that probably accounts for the gardenia in Carr's buttonhole.'

Selby whistled in surprise as he watched the tall, graceful figure of the criminal lawyer pause impressively in front of the little woman. Carr bowed and raised his hat with a deferential courtesy that transformed a casual greeting into a ceremony.

Several years ago old Alfonse Baker Carr had moved to Madison City and purchased a residence in the ultra-exclusive Orange Grove Heights district. Ostensibly, he planned to retire from his metropolitan practice, but the old maestro had remained as active as ever. It was indeed rumoured that the quiet environment of his residence in this outlying county furnished a sanctuary where the lawyer could plan those dramatic last-minute shifts in evidence which metropolitan prosecutors found so annoying and with which they were so powerless to cope. One thing was certain: whenever it came to a question of 'beating the rap,' the wise ones in a dozen coastal cities could still smile crookedly as they announced cryptically, 'It's just as easy as A B C.'

Naturally, Madison City had looked askance at this foreign element in its midst which seemed such a sinister and mysterious intrusion. But old A B C, in his richly resonant voice, had assured one and all that he looked on Madison City not as a place to carry on his profession, but only as a tranquil spot in which to drift leisurely down the remaining years of a life that had been too crowded with excitement. In fact, he hoped this wholesome environment would add another score of years at least to his life. And there was that in the dignified, courtly way the old warhorse had stated his case that gave to the community a certain feeling of reassurance, which, as events proved, had by no means been justified.

'Now what in the world do you suppose A B C wants with *her*?' Sylvia Martin asked.

'Is he alone?' Selby asked.

'Yes. He drove down to the train in his big sedan – the one that's supposed to be bullet-proof. He drove it himself ... Oh look, Doug! There's another one!'

'Another what?'

'Another gardenia.'

Selby's eyes narrowed. 'So it is. This time it's a man. Been travelling all night on the day coach, I'd say, judging from the wrinkled suit and the soiled shirt; and it's a wilted, bruised gardenia. I wonder if that's just a coincidence or whether ... No, look. Carr's signalling to him.'

Carr raised his hand, caught the man's eye and nodded.

The man, middle-aged, clad in a rumpled brown business suit, walked slowly over toward the tall criminal lawyer. An imitation leather suitcase swung against his leg as he walked.

Sylvia remarked in an undertone, 'They're something alike. I don't mean a resemblance, I mean their station in life.'

'Note a disagreement,' Selby said, his eyes twinkling. 'The woman is pure gold. The man assays fourteen carat brass.'

'I know, Doug, but he's the same type – the same – oh, you know, he looks as though he'd been pushed around a lot by life and had learned to expect it. He's probably ten years younger, but he's a man with – no, wait a minute, Doug. You're right! I can see when he smiles. It's a cunning, crafty smile. He's a scheming, petty crook masking behind that air of synthetic meekness.'

Selby said musingly, 'I'd like very much to know who they are.'

'Let's find out, Doug. I'll give old A B C a ring after a while and tell him that the paper is looking for news for its Personal Column; that I understand he has some house guests.'

'Perhaps they won't be house guests.'

'Well, he's herding them over to his automobile, putting their baggage in with them. At least it's good enough for a call and a few questions later on. Perhaps he'll tell me something.'

'Perhaps,' Selby said somewhat dubiously. 'Having lunch with me, Sylvia?'

'That's an invitation?'

'Definitely.'

'I'm a working woman, you know, Doug.'

'Am *I* not worth an interview?'

'I'll say! Will you tell us about your European experiences?'

'No comment.'

'I knew it. That's a heck of an interview.'

'A good reporter could expand that into a half column.'

'Yes,' she said laughingly, 'I think I can do just that. "Former District Attorney Selby, lean, hard and tanned, reputed to have been cited for personal bravery in action, passed through Madison City yesterday on his way to a new assignment about which he would make no comment ..." It's a date, Doug. I'll call it business. At the Orange Bowl Café at twelve-thirty.'

'Be seeing you,' he told her.

'Doug – doesn't anyone know you're coming?'

'No. I didn't tell a soul.'

'Rex Brandon will be simply tickled pink.'

'He's still sheriff?' Doug asked.

'Oh, sure.'

'How about the new district attorney?'

Sylvia Martin made a little nose-wrinkling gesture. 'Ask Rex about him. How about letting me give you a lift to the courthouse?'

'I've got some bags to attend to. I'll get a taxi later on and –'

'Better attend to your bags later on. Taxis aren't to be had just like that – not these days. There's a war on, or did you know, Major? Come on, I'll drive you up.'

CHAPTER TWO

Rex Brandon, seated at his battered desk in the Sheriff's Office, was wrestling with some of the paperwork which he found so annoying, when Selby walked in.

For several seconds the sheriff didn't look up, but gave frowning concentration to the printed blank on the desk before him.

'Just a minute,' he said over his shoulder. 'These confounded blanks. More stuff to fill in than you can shake a stick at.'

Selby smilingly watched the familiar lines of the sheriff's face, bronzed to the colour of good saddle leather, tense with annoyance as the sheriff wrestled with the red tape incident to public office.

Rex Brandon was twenty-five years older than Selby, and he had as a backlog for his official qualifications a keen knowledge of human nature and a philosophy which had all the calm dignity of the outdoors, the mountains, the stars at night – the wisdom which man acquired from observation and meditation, as distinguished from the knowledge acquired in books and colleges.

The sheriff abruptly turned in his chair, said, 'What can I do for you?' and looked at the insignia on Doug's uniform, searching for the proper military title.

'*Doug!*' he shouted. 'What in the deuce do you mean giving an old bowlegged cowpuncher a jolt like that? Why didn't you let me know you were coming?'

'No time,' Selby said.

The sheriff's left hand crashed down on Selby's shoulder with cordial impact. His right hand all but crushed Selby's. 'You're looking fine, Doug. What's new?'

'Nothing much,' Selby said, his eyes twinkling.

'No, I suppose not,' the sheriff observed sarcastically. 'Just a few citations, and you're probably mixed up to your eyebrows in work on some spy ring. But it's all just a matter of routine to you! Still smoke a pipe, Doug?'

Selby laughed. 'Haven't gone in for it much since I've been in the service. A uniform doesn't have pipe pockets.'

'I've got one of your old pipes here. Remember you used to keep one in my office, and we'd sit down and smoke out the solution to many a tough problem?'

The sheriff opened a drawer, pulled out an encrusted brier pipe.

'Got some of your favourite tobacco here, too,' the sheriff said. 'Sort of keep it moistened up with a little good rum in the humidor. Let's sit back and light up, Doug. Like old times … Gosh, I'm glad you're here!'

Rex Brandon fished a tobacco sack and cigarette papers from his pocket, held the paper curled around his forefinger and spilled tobacco into the paper.

'How's the new district attorney doing?' Selby asked.

The sheriff deliberated over that question for a moment, then said, 'Well, in a way Carl Gifford's doing all right, Doug.' Then he added, 'He's an opinionated cuss.'

'Influenced by the old Sam Roper crowd?' Selby asked, referring to the district attorney whom Selby had defeated.

10

'Well, no. Sam Roper is sort of in the background these days. He's just another lawyer. There's a new political crowd coming up. You know the war brought some industries into the county and – things change around a bit. Carl Gifford is doing all right, only I think he's getting ready to throw me to the wolves if he gets a chance between now and election time. You never feel like you're partners with him. If there's ever a slip-up, he'd save himself by making me the goat. It ain't a comfortable feeling. Wish you'd get back here and take over your old office.'

Selby laughed. 'Think Gifford would resign so I would be appointed?'

The sheriff was serious. 'No, he wouldn't,' he said bluntly. 'He's got the office and he'll hang onto it.'

'That wasn't his attitude when he was appointed following my resignation.'

'It's his attitude now.'

They were silent for a moment.

'Not that I want the job,' Selby said, laughing. 'It's high time I got out of it and stayed out.'

'I suppose,' the sheriff conceded grudgingly, 'that you've sacrificed enough to the government in one form or another, Doug. But – I sure miss you, Boy.'

'How's old A B C doing? Is he behaving himself?' Selby asked.

The sheriff ran his fingers through his thick matted hair. 'Now then,' he said, 'you're asking real questions.'

'I saw him down at the depot.'

'Speak to him?'

'No, he didn't see me. He was looking for some friends of his, evidently.'

Rex Brandon said, 'You can't tell about that old man, Doug. You never know just what he's doing.'

'He's up to something?'

The sheriff drew thoughtfully on his cigarette. 'I think he's always up to something, Doug. You were a lot more charitable with the man than I ever was.'

'I like him,' Selby admitted. 'I suppose he's unscrupulous, but he's an artist. He's at the top of his profession.'

'Such as it is,' the sheriff remarked.

Selby laughed. 'He's a criminal lawyer, Rex. He doesn't defend people who are innocent. He defends people who are charged with crime.'

'And he consistently gets them off.'

'But, Rex, can't you see that A B Carr is simply a necessary by-product of a system of justice which tries to be fair?'

'I don't get it.'

'Suppose a lawyer wouldn't represent a person whom he thought guilty?'

'The ethical lawyers won't do it.'

'All right,' Selby said, 'then you don't have a trial by jury, you have a trial by lawyer. In other words, a man finds himself involved in a case where the circumstantial evidence is black against him. He goes to lawyer after lawyer, and because they think the man is guilty they won't even consent to give him a defence. The law says a man is entitled to a trial by *jury*, not a trial by the lawyers whom he consults.'

'I s'pose so,' the sheriff conceded. 'He's mixed up in a civil suit now – some sort of a will contest. Inez Stapleton, the girl who studied law so you'd have to notice her, is on the other side.'

Selby's voice showed interest. 'Who's representing the contestant, Rex?'

'Inez is. She thinks she stands a chance on undue influence.'

Selby shook his head. 'Next to impossible to really prove …'

The telephone rang.

12

Sheriff Brandon scooped up the receiver, said, 'Sheriff's Office. Brandon speaking … Hello, Sylvia. Seen Doug? Oh, you have … Yes, he's here … Okay, I'll put him on.'

The sheriff grinned at Selby, held his hand over the mouthpiece of the telephone and said, 'Sounds like somebody else is glad to see you back. Sylvia wants to talk with you.'

Selby took the telephone, heard Sylvia's voice edged with excitement. 'Doug! We're shifting our lunch date. And can you make it right away?'

'Why … I guess so, yes. I'm just talking with Rex and …'

'Listen, Doug. I'm on the track of something. I'm at the Palm Café, and you know what's happened?'

'What?'

'A gorgeous blonde, with Hollywood stamped all over her, came in on the ten-forty-five stage. At least she told the waiter she did. She's over there at the Palm Café ordering lunch.'

'Just what,' Selby asked, 'does the gorgeous blonde have to do with our luncheon date?'

'Doug, she's wearing a corsage of white gardenias. And it may be just a hunch, but … Gosh, Doug. I don't want to let her out of my sight, and I don't want to miss my lunch date with you, and *couldn't* you come down here right now and have lunch and we could keep an eye on her?'

Selby laughed. 'Still as enthusiastic as ever, Sylvia, and still making mysteries out of people.'

'Too much imagination no doubt. I know when I was a little girl and used to play pirate cave, I got really frightened because I always just *knew* there *were* pirates in the cave. Doug, bring Rex Brandon along, and we'll have an old time reunion.'

'I'll see what I can do,' Selby said.

'But you'll come down here right away?'

'Okay.'

Selby hung up and said, 'Sylvia Martin's on the trail of a story, having to do with the most recent activities of A B C.'

'What's Carr doing now?'

'Apparently holding a convention of some sort. He doesn't know the people, and they don't know him. So they identify themselves with white gardenias.'

Brandon said, 'It's probably something connected with his city office and doesn't have anything to do with us. I think a lot of the spectacular stunts he pulls in the big city are really worked out and engineered to the finest detail here.'

'Well, Sylvia wants us to come along and have lunch down at the Palm Café where we can see the latest addition to Carr's convention, a beautiful blonde – the striking Hollywood type.'

'Wants us *both* to join her at lunch?'

'That's right.'

Brandon laughed and said, 'She wants you, Doug. But I'll drive you down.'

'Oh, come on and have lunch with us, Rex.'

The sheriff hesitated. 'I'll feel like a fifth wheel on a wagon – and the wife will certainly snort when I tell her I horned in on a lunch date with you and Sylvia.'

'Come on, Rex. It'll be like old times.'

Sheriff Brandon dropped his cigarette stub into an ashtray, pushed back the creaky swivel chair. 'I'm so darned glad to see you, I'm going to do just that,' he announced.

CHAPTER THREE

Sylvia Martin and the sheriff insisted on putting Doug Selby on the other side of the table where they could both look at him. Their luncheon booth was almost directly across from the booth where a blonde woman was slowly and thoughtfully eating a very light lunch.

'She certainly doesn't belong in Madison City,' Brandon said.

'I'll say she doesn't,' Sylvia Martin said. 'And I can tell you just about all there is to know about her from a woman's viewpoint. You strip her of those trappings and she wouldn't be so breath-taking. But that scenery cost lots of money, boys. That fur is worth around fifteen hundred dollars. Notice the diamond on her right hand and the earrings. That complexion is worked over by experts every day. That figure is carefully kept in line by diet and exercise, the lines are skilfully brought out by clothes that weren't just picked up any old place. She puts in more time, more thought and more effort on that body of hers than the average woman puts in on cooking for her husband, keeping her house, raising a family of children, putting up fruit in season, and doing work for church socials, Red Cross drives, Community Chests and …'

'Stop it,' Brandon interrupted laughingly. 'You make me dizzy.'

'I mean it – every word of it,' Sylvia said. 'That woman's body is her career.'

Brandon thought that over. 'That's a delicate way of expressing it.'

'I don't mean it in any way except just what I said. She puts in her time and effort thinking of herself. And when a woman has invested so much time and energy in preserving her appearance, she usually wants to … oh, oh!'

Sylvia Martin was seated where she could see the door, and as she stopped with a little exclamation, Brandon asked, 'What is it, Sylvia?'

'Old A B C,' she said, 'my hunch was right.'

Carr entered the restaurant casually, as though merely in search of a vacant booth where he could have lunch. He strolled along with that calm, impressive dignity which is associated with conscious power, then suddenly his eyes lit on the gardenia corsage and he stopped.

For a moment the blonde didn't look up. When she did, there was only mild interest in her eyes.

Then Carr took two steps forward, bent solicitously over the table and said something in a low voice.

The blonde smiled, gave him her hand.

Carr sat down. He said nothing for a matter of two or three seconds, during which the woman opposite sized him up with the calmly calculating expression of a prospective purchaser appraising property which has been offered for sale.

Sylvia Martin said, 'There goes my nice theory.'

'What theory?' Brandon asked.

'About the people who wear white gardenias and with whom Carr is keeping such a mysterious rendezvous. I had been telling Doug at the train that they were all alike – at least in their general station in life – people who had been pushed around, beaten down and now this hothouse flower enters the picture. Life never pushed *that* woman around!'

16

Some psychic sensitivity made Carr turn quickly, catching Sylvia Martin's eyes regarding him with ill-concealed interest.

Selby suddenly laughed. 'Caught in the act, Sylvia.'

She had jerked her eyes away and now started talking vivaciously about nothing in particular.

Selby shook his head. 'You're not fooling him any, Sylvia.' Nor was she.

For a moment Carr hesitated, then, in his richly resonant voice, said to his companion, 'Excuse me a moment, please.' With every semblance of cordial friendship, he arose and approached the other booth.

'Good morning Miss Martin,' he said, 'and Sheriff Brandon. How are you? I don't see you very often these days.'

He turned to Doug Selby, apparently seeing only a man in uniform and wishing to include him in the conversation with a smile.

Suddenly, recognition came to his eyes. 'Why, Doug Selby!' he exclaimed. 'Pardon me, *Major* Selby. This is indeed a pleasure!'

His hand shot forward.

Doug got to his feet, gripped Carr's muscular hand.

The criminal lawyer was somewhere in the fifties, big-boned, lean, magnetic, his wavy hair touched with grey, eyebrows inclined to be bushy, but his face with its high cheekbones, firm jaw and clean-cut features, was unmistakably stamped with character and ability. 'Are you back for good?' he asked.

'Just a furlough,' Selby told him. 'Thought I'd stop over and see how the county was coming along.'

'We miss you,' Carr said gravely, and his face had become an expressionless mask. It was as though Selby's presence in Madison City constituted a major complication which Carr wanted to consider carefully, and his face, schooled by years of experience, had automatically disassociated itself from the man's thought.

'You're still practising?' Sylvia asked.

Carr made a deprecatory gesture that had behind it both grace and dignity. 'Nothing to speak of. I'm trying to retire. I want to spend my time in your delightful community enjoying the friendly atmosphere ... But, of course ...' He finished the sentence with just the faintest shrug of his shoulders.

Selby's eyes twinkled at the adroit way the old lawyer had avoided the question without seeming to be other than frank and friendly.

'I presume,' Sylvia Martin said, glancing surreptitiously at the blonde in the opposite booth, who was watching the progress of the conversation with the same calm appraisal with which she had studied old A B C, 'many of your clients from the city don't like to have you retire.'

'You flatter me,' Carr said.

'And therefore follow you here with their problems.'

Abruptly Carr threw back his head and laughed, a deeply rich, resonant laugh. 'Such commendable loyalty to your employers, Miss Martin,' he said. 'And when you see them, will you convey my compliments and tell them that whenever A B C has a story release for publication he most certainly will bear in mind the *Madison City Clarion*. And now if you will excuse me. But it certainly was a pleasure to see you, Major. And now that you're no longer in office, I trust our association may be a little – well, shall we say less formal?'

'I'm afraid there won't be much association,' Selby said. 'I'm leaving for San Francisco in a few days.'

This time Carr's face betrayed itself. The information quite evidently meant something to the criminal lawyer. The lines of the features didn't change, but the eyes did. They lit up with a sudden interest which was instantly veiled by a conscious effort.

'And from there?' Carr asked courteously.

'South Pacific, probably.'

Carr said almost sadly, 'Any time you wish *really* to capitalize upon your legal ability, Counsellor, you won't have any trouble finding satisfactory connections ... I presume there would be no interest to you in considering an association in the city with an older man?'

His eyes regarded Selby gravely.

'I'm afraid not. I like this place.'

'I can't blame you, Major. I can't blame you in the least. I like it myself. I only wish I could find some younger man who had your keen insight into the law ... However, this is hardly the time or the place – if you'll excuse me. I certainly hope I get to see you again, Major.'

And Carr, bowing gravely, crossed back to rejoin his companion.

'That,' Sylvia Martin said, 'was a very courteous rebuke. I feel as though I'd been mentally spanked for staring across at something that's none of my business.'

'You have,' Selby said. 'We all have, and it was done very nicely. How old is she, Sylvia?'

'Past thirty.'

'Heavens, no!' Brandon exclaimed. 'She can't be past twenty-seven.'

'Notice her hands – and her eyes,' Sylvia insisted.

'Let's not,' Selby laughed. 'At least, let's not get caught at it.'

Sylvia swung around so her shoulder furnished a screen. 'You're right, Doug. Let's talk about something else. They're going out! That simplifies things. Now tell us about yourself, Doug.'

CHAPTER FOUR

The waitress was just taking the dessert orders when Sylvia Martin, sitting where she could look down the aisle, said, 'I'll bet he's looking for you.'

'What is it?' Brandon asked. 'Who's looking?'

'Frank Norwalk, proprietor of the Madison Hotel. And if he isn't – yes, here he comes.'

'The sheriff here?' Norwalk asked, then suddenly realizing that he had an audience lowered his voice. 'Sheriff, I wonder if … Why hello, Doug Selby! How are you?'

Selby shook hands.

'Back for long?' Norwalk asked.

'Just for a few days.'

Norwalk nodded, apparently too preoccupied with his own affairs to pay very much attention to Selby's answer. He shifted his eyes back to the sheriff, said, 'A little trouble over at the hotel, Sheriff.'

'Okay,' Brandon said. 'I'll come over as soon as I finish lunch. Sit down, Frank, and have some dessert with us.'

'No, thank you … it's … I'm afraid it's urgent, Sheriff.'

The sheriff said, 'Okay, I'll be with you. If you'll excuse me, Doug.'

'Go right ahead,' Selby said.

'Sorry to break up the luncheon,' Norwalk apologized.

'Quite all right.'

'Well, I'll be seeing you, Doug,' Brandon said, and followed Norwalk out of the café.

'I wonder,' Sylvia Martin said musingly, 'just what the trouble is. I think in my professional capacity I'll drift over that way, Doug.'

'Strange he didn't call the city authorities,' Selby said.

'That's what I was thinking.'

'Is Otto Larkin still Chief of Police?'

'Sure. He knows how to flim-flam the voters. He's the same old back-slapper, only now he's changed his attitude toward the county officials. He just bubbles co-operation and good will for the Sheriff's Office. Every time he ... wait a minute, Doug. Here's Rex Brandon coming back.'

The sheriff's walk was more rapid and more businesslike now. He moved back to the booth, bent over and said in a low voice, 'Doug, Norwalk didn't tell me until we got to the door. A man's dropped dead over there under rather mysterious circumstances. Thought you and Sylvia might like to come over.'

'I would,' Sylvia said promptly. 'I want the story.'

Selby hesitated. 'After all, Rex, I'd just be horning in on things. I don't want to ...'

'Oh, come on,' Brandon urged. 'Things are different now from what they used to be. Otto Larkin is very friendly. It's just a routine that won't keep us very long. The man dropped dead from heart failure in his room. But he'd been acting sort of funny, and Norwalk wants to be in the clear on the thing.'

'Please come, Doug,' Sylvia urged.

Selby surrendered, paid the luncheon check and took Sylvia Martin's arm as they walked out of the restaurant to where Norwalk was waiting on the sidewalk.

'It isn't anything,' Norwalk said nervously, 'only I didn't want to touch the body or move anything in the room until everyone had had a chance to – well, you know, make certain everything was all right.'

'That's quite right,' Brandon said.

'He evidently wasn't feeling well. He'd ordered breakfast sent up to his room, had a spell with his heart somewhere in the middle of a meal.'

'Did you get his name from the register?'

'Yes. Fred Roff from Los Angeles.'

'What room?'

'Six-nineteen.'

'Well, we'll all go on up.'

Norwalk said, 'It's rather – well, it isn't particularly pleasant. I thought that Miss Martin, perhaps …'

Sylvia said, 'If it's the publicity you're worried about, don't run up a temperature. We'll handle it in the usual way, stating that a body was found in a "downtown hotel". Not that that will fool anybody, but …'

'I know, I know,' Norwalk interrupted hastily. 'But if you don't mention the name of the hotel, it makes it lots better. The Los Angeles papers might copy your stuff, and if they mention the name of the hotel …'

'Don't worry,' Sylvia reassured him.

They entered the hotel and went across to the elevator.

'Sixth?' the operator asked.

Norwalk nodded and said, 'And don't stop for anyone on the way up.'

'The city police up there?' Brandon asked.

'I don't know, Sheriff. I told the clerk to get Chief Larkin and ask him to come up right away. I rang the courthouse myself and they said you were out at lunch. I thought I might find you across the street.'

Brandon nodded.

The elevator stopped at the sixth floor. The elevator operator said in a low voice, 'The police haven't arrived yet, Mr Norwalk.'

'We'll go right on in,' Norwalk said, taking a pass-key from his pocket. 'When the chief comes, show him in.'

Norwalk led the way down to 619, opened the door with his pass-key and stood back to one side. 'There you are,' he said. 'Nothing has been touched.'

Brandon stopped just inside the doorway. Sylvia Martin and Selby stood at his side.

'This just the way it was?' Brandon asked.

'Just exactly the way the maid found it.'

'The bed hasn't been slept in.'

'No, he registered about eight-thirty this morning.'

The sheriff turned to Selby, raised his eyes questioningly. The breakfast things on the table gave a garish tone to the entire scene. The light which streamed in through the south window was reflected from silvered dish covers, coffee pot, cream pitcher, and emphasized the crisp freshness of the white tablecloth.

The man who lay sprawled on the floor had evidently tumbled from a chair which had been drawn up in front of the breakfast table. In his left hand he held a stained napkin. Coffee had spilled from the overturned cup to make a splotch on the tablecloth. Apparently, the metal covers had not been removed from the food.

The little group stood for a moment awkwardly ill at ease, regarding the dead man with that hushed futility which is the instinctive reaction of the living to the dead. Then self-consciously at first, but gradually with more assurance, they began the routine survey of the premises which was the first preliminary step in their investigations.

'Let's look around, but be careful not to touch anything,' Sheriff Brandon said. 'Looks as though he'd had a spell of heart attack all right – just as he was getting ready to eat.'

The dead man was rather tall and rangy, a man who might have been sixty-one or sixty-two. His dark hair had turned grey. The coarse moustache was close-clipped. His bifocal spectacles had been pushed into one-sided incongruity by his fall and in some strange way lent an oddly facetious note to the occasion, as though these man-made aids to vision were somehow jeering at the final destiny of the eyes they had served.

The man's clothes were of good quality but possessed a certain ready-made lack of individuality and were badly in need of pressing. The skin at the back of the neck was checkerboarded with a mesh of coarse wrinkles. His hands, which had been strong and powerful in life, showed no signs of physical labour.

Selby moved over to inspect the breakfast things on the table. 'One lump of sugar on a small saucer here,' he said to the proprietor of the hotel.

Norwalk nodded. 'We don't send up a sugar bowl any more with breakfast service in a room. We found that we'd send it up full of sugar cubes and it would come back empty. And now we send up sugar cubes in a little saucer – three to an order of coffee.'

Selby said, 'Evidently the man poured himself a cup of coffee, drank it and then became ill. Apparently he didn't even remove the covers from the other plates.'

'That's right,' Norwalk said, and then added, 'I guess you can have a heart stroke about any time – playing golf, sleeping or eating.'

'Did he give any street address?' Selby asked.

'No. We don't always require that on the register. There's a blank on the registration card where guests are supposed to fill in a street number, but sometimes the clerks get careless and this *would* have to be one of those times.'

'Did he wire ahead for a reservation?'

'No, just came in about eight-thirty this morning and asked if we had a room.'

'Baggage?' Selby asked.

Norwalk nodded to the one handbag and a somewhat battered briefcase over on the stand reserved for baggage.

'He was travelling light. Just the briefcase, the bag and his overcoat. I checked on that with the bellboy.'

Rex Brandon prowled around the room, said, 'Well, I guess that's about all there is to it but we'll have the Doc look him over. He ...'

Knuckles pounded a loud and peremptory summons on the door.

'Otto Larkin,' the sheriff said laconically.

Frank Norwalk unlocked the door.

Otto Larkin pushed it open, barely glanced at the dead man on the floor, shifted his eyes to the sheriff, said, 'Hello, Rex, how they coming?'

Norwalk closed and locked the door.

Larkin turned to Doug Selby, attempted to correlate the familiar face and the unaccustomed uniform, then grabbed Selby's hand.

'Doug Selby! Boy, I certainly am glad to see you! I really am glad,' and then in the manner of one who has become accustomed to having his sincerity doubted, added, 'I really mean it.'

During the first part of Selby's term of office, while the paunchy Chief of Police had been outwardly cordial, there had been no doubt that his political sympathies had lain with Sam Roper and the ousted regime. Behind a guise of personal cordiality there had lurked the deadly knife of political enmity ready to be plunged into either the sheriff or the district attorney, or both, as occasion presented itself. Now, with the complete turnabout which the professional politician sees only as a perfectly natural readjustment, Larkin was bidding for the friendship of these two men.

'So it's *Major* Selby now,' Larkin went on, his face genial with good humour.

'How is everything?' Selby asked. 'You're looking well.'

'Feeling fine,' Larkin said. 'Carrying a little too much weight, but I'm going to take some of it off. What have we got here?'

Norwalk said, 'A man keeled over with heart failure.'

Larkin glanced once more at the dead man on the floor, then tossed off his verdict. 'Bum ticker, all right. Okay, we've looked it over. S'pose we've got to notify the coroner. Well, that covers things for us here. How about going downstairs and having a cup of coffee, boys, and …'

Selby said, 'Take a look at this lump of sugar, Rex.'

'What's wrong with it?'

'See if you smell anything. And notice that it seems slightly damp. Notice the way it glistens.'

Sheriff Brandon looked at the lump of sugar.

'What about the sugar lump?' Otto Larkin asked.

Selby said, 'Notice that peculiar froth that came from the man's lips. Bend over him and you get the slight odour of the oil of bitter almonds.'

'What's that got to do with it?'

'It's benzaldehyde and is characteristic of poisoning by hydrocyanic acid, or cyanide of potassium, and, just in case that remaining sugar lump has been soaked in cyanide of potassium, you'll find that the slight tendency to absorb moisture from the air is characteristic.'

Norwalk frowned, his manner contained dignified irritation. Otto Larkin's little eyes were glittering with interest now, and the sheriff was grave.

Sylvia Martin asked softly, 'You think it was suicide, Doug?'

'I can't see why a man would want to go to all that trouble to commit suicide. If he wanted to take poison why didn't he just take it and be done with it? He ...'

Once more knuckles tapped against the panels of the door. Norwalk glanced inquiringly at the sheriff, then without waiting for a signal unlocked the door and opened it.

A bellboy stood in the hallway, holding in his hand a small oblong package wrapped in a green paper. 'Thought you might like this,' he said.

'What is it?' Norwalk asked.

'Package came for Mr Roff in this room. We tried to deliver it and got no answer, so we left a note in the key box that there was a package for him ...'

'What time?' Sheriff Brandon asked.

'The note shows it was nine-thirty a.m.'

'What'll we do?' Norwalk asked. 'Open it?'

The sheriff nodded.

Norwalk untied the string, removed the green paper and disclosed a white cardboard box. He raised the cover from the box and then frowned as he inspected the contents. 'What the heck was the guy doing – ordering his own flowers?' he asked.

'What is it?' Brandon asked.

By way of answer, Norwalk held the box up so that the others could see the contents.

In the interior of the box, nestled against a background of crumpled green paper, so that the flower would not become bruised in handling, was a single white gardenia.

Sylvia Martin's fingers dug into Selby's arm, pleading with him for silence.

Brandon asked crisply, 'How did it happen that flower was sent over here? Did he order it himself or …'

'I guess he ordered it himself,' Norwalk said. 'I had his phone calls checked before you folks came over. One of his calls was to the florist. Right after he checked in.'

'One of them?' Selby asked. 'Was there another?'

'Yeah, he called the depot at eight fifty-five.'

'The depot,' Brandon said. '… they may remember the call.'

'I already checked on that,' Norwalk told him. 'There was only one man in the office at that time. He says he remembered the call because he took it just before the fast freight, Number Nine, came in. He says this call was from a man who wanted to know if Number Twenty-three was apt to be on time.'

'Number Twenty-three,' Brandon said to Selby. 'That was the train you came on.'

Selby said quite casually, 'And about a dozen other passengers.'

Sylvia Martin's eyes were pleading with Rex Brandon. When she saw that he had caught their message, she glanced warningly toward Otto Larkin.

'Did he have any visitors?' Selby asked Norwalk.

'No, I checked on that. No visitors and no other calls.'

Brandon said, 'I think we'll all get out of here and we'll have some fingerprints taken.'

'Sure,' Larkin said easily. 'I was just going to suggest that myself.'

'Who has the adjoining rooms?' Selby asked.

'I don't know,' Norwalk told him. 'I'll have to look them up on the register.'

'They're occupied?'

'I think so.'

The sheriff said, 'Let's go take a look at the register. It might be important to see who has the adjoining rooms.'

'Oh, have a heart,' Norwalk pleaded.

'Just routine,' Otto Larkin reassured him, clapping a heavy hand on the worried hotel proprietor's shoulder.

Norwalk opened the door. They filed out into the corridor, then suddenly stopped as they heard the sound of a bolt snapping back on the door of the adjoining room.

The door opened. The blonde who had been talking with A B Carr at the restaurant stepped out into the hallway, gave the little group the benefit of an inspection with a haughty air of impersonal disdain, then pulled the door shut, twisted the key and swept on down toward the elevator.

CHAPTER FIVE

'Who is she?' Brandon asked the hotel proprietor.

'The woman who just went down the hall?'

'Yes.'

'Lord, I don't know. She's evidently in six-seventeen. Please, let's keep our heads.'

'I've seen her before,' Sylvia said by way of explanation. 'Let's go and take a look at the register.'

'Okay, okay,' Norwalk said wearily, and then added, 'if you think a hotel keeper hasn't got his troubles, what with the linen shortage, the laundry tie-ups, the poor help and the increase in travel, you have another guess coming.'

Larkin said soothingly, 'That's right. That's right. Tell you what, folks; anything we can do to make things easier for Norwalk we should do.'

'What would you suggest?' Brandon asked dryly.

Larkin could think of no answer to that question.

They rode down in the elevator, consulted the register, and found that the blonde's name was Anita Eldon and that her residence was Hollywood; that she had checked into room six-seventeen while the sheriff's little group had been examining the body and the surroundings in 619.

'So you see,' Norwalk said, 'you just *can't* go around attributing significance to every little thing that happens in a hotel. A hotel is a peculiar place. All sorts of people come from all over the country on all sorts of business, and you just have to take them the way you find them. About all you can do is make certain rules that keep your place from becoming a dump.'

'Who had the room before this blonde checked in?' Brandon asked.

'The records show that an Irving W Jerome, of Los Angeles, had occupied the room. And Irving Jerome had also failed to give any street address when he registered.'

Sylvia Martin said to Selby, 'Well, I'm going to try and hunt up those others – the flowers, you know.'

Selby said, 'Luck. I'll visit around. See you later, Sylvia.'

Harry Perkins, the coroner, rather slender, spare of frame, with high cheekbones and a perpetually jovial disposition, showed up to take charge of the body.

Sheriff Brandon started a routine investigation. Otto Larkin bubbled verbal co-operation, and Sylvia Martin started off on the trail of the other two white gardenias, leaving Doug Selby free to wander off on his own.

It was exactly twelve-thirty when Doug Selby climbed the one flight of stairs and walked down the long corridor to the door which bore the legend INEZ STAPLETON, *Attorney at Law*. ENTER.

Selby entered the office, saw that the stenographer was out to lunch, that the door to the private office was open. Without much expectation of finding Inez in, he walked over to look through the door.

Inez was seated at her desk. Law books were piled high around her, and as Selby watched, she pulled a pad of legal foolscap toward her and started scribbling excerpts from the law book she was reading.

For several seconds Selby stood watching her profile, the concentration of her eyes, the intellectual forehead that indicated a capacity for thought, the straight, delicate nose, the feminine mouth, the smooth lines of her chin and throat. The light caught and reflected the highlights of deeply-waved hair.

She suddenly paused in the middle of her writing, glanced up over her shoulder, frowned with annoyance, then swung around in her swivel chair for a better look.

Selby saw her eyes widen with surprise. For a moment the colour drained from her face. Then it was flushed and dark. But there was a dignity in her manner as she came toward him.

'Why, Doug!' she exclaimed, started to say something else, then stopped.

Selby stood with both her hands in his.

'Hello, Counsellor,' he said, grinning.

Her eyes were hungry. She said nothing, but abruptly raised her face, and Selby felt the warm, tremulous caress of her lips, and then she was away from him, laughing nervously.

'Heavens, Doug. I'm getting sentimental – for a veteran counsellor.'

Selby looked at the big desk. 'Rather work than eat?' he asked.

'I guess so. I'm terribly interested in what I'm doing. I have a will contest case coming up for trial tomorrow. However, I suppose I should take on a little nourishment.'

She hesitated.

For a moment, it seemed that the silence could become awkward.

Selby said easily, 'I have had an early lunch, Inez, but I'd like to run down and sit with you if you want to eat.'

Her chin was up, her manner suddenly crisply professional. 'No, never mind, Doug. I should stay here anyway. Do sit down and let's talk.'

'You're busy,' he told her.

'Please.'

Selby dropped into the big client's chair by the side of the desk.

'Tell me about it,' he said.

'Tell me about you, Doug.'

'Nothing to tell. I'm home on a brief furlough. Going to San Francisco, then out from there. Want to talk about the case?'

'Do I!' she exclaimed. 'Doug, I feel absolutely lost! I'm starving for someone whom I can trust and with whom I can discuss the thing. Old A B Carr is on the other side, and when you're fighting him you have the most peculiar feeling of futility. You just don't feel that you're getting anywhere near the man. It's as though you were having one of those nightmares where you run and run, and move your legs but can't seem to gain an inch.'

Selby said, 'I know. He's baffling.'

'It's more than that. You feel that you're up against some sort of a system, something that's unbeatable. You try to hit, and there's nothing there to hit. And yet you can feel it all about you, closing in on you, smothering you …'

Selby laughed. 'You've been studying too hard, Inez.'

Her smile was wan. 'I suppose so. And it doesn't do any good. The more I study, the more forlorn my case seems.'

'You're representing the contestants?'

'Yes. One of them.'

'Who's the other?'

'A brother represented by some attorney in the Midwest. He's supposed to arrive late tonight and we shall have a conference. Somehow, his letters haven't been too reassuring. I gather that he's a rule-of-thumb lawyer who won't be educated on the fine points of the law.'

'What *are* the fine points?' Selby asked, grinning.

'Lots of them. I suppose our only chance is on the ground of undue influence, and it seems that's almost impossible to prove. You have to prove that the undue influence existed at the exact moment that the will was signed. And of course there are subscribing witnesses who will testify that everything was quite all right, all shipshape and above board.'

'You think they will?'

'Oh, of course. They've already signed a statement which was a part of the will -- an attestation clause stating that the will was duly and regularly executed. You can't expect them to go back on their signed statement, and by the time old A B Carr gets done with them they'll remember all the little details, all the facial expressions, everything that was said. Carr drew the will in his Los Angeles office.'

'Can't you find some better ground than undue influence?'

'I'm afraid not. I'm contesting on every ground under the sun, but when it comes to a showdown, we'll have to win or lose on the strength of undue influence.'

'But you can show that by circumstantial evidence.'

'Yes, I know. We can show a lot of things that happened, a lot of things that could have happened. We can show circumstances that are very, very suspicious. But, in the long run, the proof must go to the exact moment that the will was signed. At that moment, there was present the lawyer who drew the will, two subscribing witnesses, and the decedent. And no one else.'

'How about the person who did the influencing?'

'She was in another room. Of course, old Alfonse Baker Carr was smart enough to handle it that way.'

'How much can you tell me about this will contest without betraying the confidence of your client?' Selby asked.

'Quite a bit, Doug. Eleanor Preston was a very wealthy woman. She lived here and had all her property here. She was never married, and left no relatives when she died, other than Barbara Honcutt, a widowed sister, who lives in Kansas, and Hervey Preston, a brother who also lives in Kansas. All of them are in the sixties. The brother was the oldest, then came Eleanor Preston, then Barbara. Eleanor was rather eccentric and crotchety, but they got along all right until about two years ago when Eleanor employed a Martha Otley as a housekeeper and travelling companion. Almost instantly, the whole picture began to change.

'Ostensibly, Martha Otley was *most* devoted to her employer, but gradually she insinuated herself into such a position of confidence that she was virtually running everything. And, about that time, Eleanor Preston began to show a desire to get out from under the burden of making decisions. Of course, most of that had been carefully cultivated by Martha Otley, but the probabilities are that Eleanor's illness had something to do with it.'

'The brother and sister were disinherited?' Selby asked.

'Cut off with one hundred dollars each.'

'What's the amount of the estate?'

'Somewhere around a million dollars. It will be a juicy plum all around.'

'I'll say so. So Eleanor Preston died, and now Martha Otley is trying to hold under a will which was …'

'Not so fast, Doug,' Inez Stapleton said. 'They both died.'

'How did it happen?'

'An automobile accident. I guess there was quite a bit of feeling in the family, and I know there had been some correspondence between Barbara Honcutt and her brother. Last year Barbara and her brother came out to visit Eleanor. Apparently they were getting some place, but Martha Otley managed to out-general them, and the first thing anyone knew, Eleanor left abruptly on a trip by airplane to Mexico. She left Barbara and Hervey just sitting here.'

'Holding the sack?' Selby asked, smiling.

'Holding the sack,' Inez said. 'Eleanor wrote them some apparently affectionate letters telling them that she felt the need of travel because she had suddenly become very nervous and wanted to go to some foreign country where she didn't know anyone and so could have a complete rest and relaxation. Of course, you can read between the lines and see what happened.'

'Where did she die?' Selby asked.

'She was visiting in McKeesville, Kansas. Martha Otley had a sister there, a Helen Elizabeth Corning, and they had gone to visit Mrs Corning.'

'Married?' Selby asked.

'A widow.'

'And Eleanor died there?'

'Near there, some town called Olympus. I'd never heard of it. Mrs Corning was driving the car. There was a blow-out and they hit the kerb and then a lamp-post. Mrs Corning was hurt, Eleanor Preston killed almost instantly, and Martha Otley died a short time later.'

Selby's eyes showed his interest. 'And I suppose that Helen Elizabeth Corning was then the heir to the entire fortune …'

'No, Martha Otley left a daughter in Nebraska who seems to spend time, too, in Hollywood. She stands to inherit the entire fortune. Helen Elizabeth Corning doesn't stand to gain a dollar – at least on the face of things.'

'You've got a tough case, Inez.'

'I know it.'

'You may get the sympathy of a jury, but when the judge instructs them that undue influence has to be proven to have existed at the very moment the signature was affixed to the will, and that a testator can dispose of his property any way he wants to, utilizing any whim or fancy that he may have, you'll be licked. Under the law you have the burden of proving not only an undue influence, but that that undue influence affected the hand of the testator at the very moment the pen signed her name to the will, and you're going to find the jury will reluctantly bring in an adverse decision. Not that I want to discourage you, but you certainly must know what you're up against.'

'I do, Doug. Of course, I'm relying on the impression the parties will make on the witness stand. I've never met Helen Elizabeth Corning, but I gather she's a shrewd schemer, and Martha Otley most certainly was. Of course, the fact that she died makes it very difficult to bring out our proof. It puts us in the position of smearing a dead woman.'

Selby nodded.

'Anyway,' Inez said, smiling, 'it's going to be a good fight, and it's going to be a savage fight. We can't afford to pull any punches. We've got to go in there and show Martha Otley for just what she was.'

'Just what was she?'

Inez Stapleton's mouth became hard. 'She was a shrewd, scheming adventuress. She had been a housekeeper, but she hadn't actually done any work for ten years. Then she found out that Eleanor Preston was alone, and through some sort of a build-up, she insinuated herself into Eleanor Preston's good graces, and then she went to work. And how she worked! Until she had things the way she wanted them, she kept the house as neat as a pin. She did all the cooking, all the washing.'

'The daughter have anything to do with her getting the job?' Selby asked.

'I don't know, Doug, apparently mother and daughter weren't very close.'

'Is she married?'

'She had been married and divorced.'

'What's her name?'

'Anita Eldon ... Why, Doug Selby! What's the matter?'

Selby said, 'I guess there's nothing to it – I've just come from the Madison Hotel. A man was found dead in room six-nineteen about an hour and a half ago. The woman who now has the adjoining room is Anita Eldon. She didn't check in until long after the man had died, but there's one peculiar circumstance that seems to tie the whole group of people up together.'

'What is it, Doug?'

Hastily Selby outlined the story of the white gardenias.

Inez Stapleton picked up a pencil from the desk, started twisting it nervously in her fingers. 'Oh, Doug,' she said almost in a whisper, 'we've *got* to find out about it. We simply must find out about it. It could be a break. I've always felt that there was something in this case if I could only put my finger on it. That's why I told you it was such a bewildering sensation fighting old A B Carr. I know just as well as you do that we haven't got a legal leg to stand on when it comes to the will contest. We haven't any real proof. We can only show things by inference, and inference isn't going to be enough. And all the while you have the feeling that old A B C is sitting back there, grinning sardonically and carefully pushing all of the real evidence into the background, leaving us with only the chaff instead of the wheat. Doug, there has to be some connection. There simply has to be. Tell me what I can do.'

Selby shook his head and said, 'I don't know, Inez. Rex Brandon is going to investigate the death. He's working on it right now.'

'Was it a murder?'

Selby said thoughtfully, 'I'm inclined to think that it was, Inez.'

'But why? Why was the man murdered? Why did he want that gardenia?'

Selby said, 'There's only one explanation I can think of, Inez. The two people who came on the train and who wore white gardenias were people that Carr didn't know. Otherwise, he wouldn't have used the white gardenia as a means of identification.'

She nodded.

'Therefore,' Selby went on, 'they must have been people who had something in common, who meant something to him. Yet, obviously, they didn't know each other. Now, it's not beyond the bounds of possibility, Inez, that they were witnesses to something in connection with that will case.'

Inez frowned.

Selby went on, 'The man who was killed in the hotel *might* have been the one who had originally summoned those witnesses. He may have been intending to put on a white gardenia and go down to the train to meet them. And it's quite possible those witnesses might have testified something that would be adverse to the interests of Carr's client ... And some way Carr found out what was going to happen and put on a white gardenia, and went down and grabbed off the witnesses ...'

'But if they're witnesses to something,' Inez asked, 'why would Anita Eldon have come to town wearing a white gardenia?'

'You've got me,' Selby said. 'I've just been thinking out loud, Inez.'

'What sort of a girl is this Anita Eldon?'

Selby said, 'Class a million. The hothouse flower type. Groomed down to the last false eyelash. She registered as being from Hollywood, not from Nebraska – she looks like Hollywood.'

'You haven't told me the name of the man who was murdered, Doug.'

'Fred Roff,' Selby said. 'He registered from Los Angeles.'

Abruptly Inez Stapleton pushed back the law books. 'I'm groping around in the dark, Doug. Be a good boy and run along. Let me see if I can think out some answers.'

CHAPTER SIX

Doug Selby found Rex Brandon in conference with Harry Perkins at the latter's undertaking parlour, the back room of which served as a morgue for Madison County. The sheriff's forehead was puckered into lines of thought.

'What's new?' Selby asked.

The sheriff said grimly, 'It *could* be murder.'

'What happened?'

'You called the turn, Doug. That remaining lump of sugar seems to be pretty well saturated with hydrocyanic acid. The doctor says it looks as though the cause of death was hydrocyanic poisoning. There wasn't any poison anywhere else in the room. Carl Gifford wants to arrest the waiter.'

'On what evidence?' Selby asked.

'That's just it. He wants to arrest him first and browbeat the evidence out of him. I don't like it.'

Selby lowered his voice, said, 'Look here, Rex, I don't want to stick my neck out on this and I'm not particularly anxious to have it get around but there's a chance that this is tied in in some way with that will contest case that comes up for trial tomorrow. There's somewhere around a million dollars involved in that and some of Carr's clients would do a lot for a million dollars.'

'What makes you think so, Doug? That it's tied up with the will contest case, I mean?'

'Those white gardenias, Rex. Anita Eldon, who has room six-seventeen, the one right next to that occupied by the dead man, is Carr's client in that will case.'

'We've made a little investigation there,' Brandon said. 'She came into town on the eleven o'clock bus and went directly to the restaurant and got something to eat. Old A B Carr met her there. She went to the hotel after we got there and was put in the adjoining room because at the moment it was the only room that was vacant. There doesn't seem to be any connection.'

'Except that white gardenia,' Selby said.

'Except the gardenia,' Brandon admitted, 'and somehow you just can't say anything about that gardenia business to Carl Gifford. It isn't the sort of stuff he'd listen to. I wonder how Sylvia's making out?'

'I don't know. I haven't heard anything from her. I've been up talking with Inez Stapleton.'

Brandon said, 'Here comes Carl Gifford now. He may not be too glad to see you.'

Gifford came bustling into the mortuary, but contrary to the sheriff's prediction, seemed very glad indeed to see the former district attorney back in Madison City.

'How are you, Mr Selby? *Major* Selby. It's really good to see you back, Major. I understand you're just stopping in for a few days before taking off for parts unknown.'

'That's right,' Selby said, shaking hands.

Gifford was thirty-two, a stocky, bull-necked, driving individual, lashed by personal and political ambition, and prone to cover up a lack of thought by reaching instantaneous, brusque decisions, and then lunging ahead, relying upon the sheer force of his charge to smash all obstacles in front of him.

'Be very glad to have you give us the benefit of any thoughts you have on this case – unofficially, of course.'

'Thank you,' Selby said. 'I haven't any.'

41

'Of course, the evidence isn't all in yet,' Gifford said, 'but there's one inescapable conclusion. The man telephoned down and ordered breakfast. We've located the waiter who took the tray up to him, Henry L Farley. It's up to the waiter to take the lumps of sugar out of the sugar container, put them on a saucer, and send them up. They don't send up sugar bowls any more. Farley is trying to cover up. He says he doesn't remember much about this particular order. He just took it up and knocked and this man opened the door. He's certain it was this man and that he was alone in the room.'

'Would he have had any motive for murdering Fred Roff?' Selby asked.

'Of course he would,' Gifford snapped, 'otherwise he wouldn't have done it. Of course we don't know what that motive is yet.'

Selby nodded his head as though Gifford had delivered himself of some statement involving a profound thought. 'That's right. You have to find out who the man is before you can find out who would have had a motive for murdering him.'

'I'm not so sure about that,' Gifford said. 'We're taking Farley up to the jail to question him. Once the doors of the jail close on him, he'll begin to weaken. They always do, except the hardened criminals.'

Selby said to Brandon, 'Just as a matter of curiosity, I'd like to take a look at what was in the bag and briefcase.'

'Perkins has got them all spread out in there,' Brandon said. 'The doctor's going to work on the body, so you'll have to sit in on the post mortem if you want to see that, Doug, but the man's things are all spread out in there. Go take a look at them.'

'Thanks, I will.'

'You don't want to come up and listen to what Farley has to say?' Gifford invited cordially.

'No, thank you,' Selby said. 'I'll just take a look at those things. You know how it is. I can't seem to dismiss the matter from my mind and …'

'Certainly, certainly,' Gifford interrupted with booming cordiality. 'Go right ahead. Help yourself, Major. Anything you want. We're glad to have your assistance. Mighty glad to get any ideas you might have. Aren't we, Sheriff?'

Brandon nodded wordlessly.

'My own idea,' Gifford went on, 'is that we'll have a confession out of Farley before night. Come on, Sheriff, let's go give him the works. I've got a court reporter ready to take down everything he says in shorthand. He's shivering in his boots right now.'

Brandon glanced over his shoulder at Doug Selby, hesitated as though searching for some excuse by which he could remain, then finding none, went out with the new district attorney.

Selby, accompanied by Harry Perkins, went on back to a room where the contents of the briefcase and the leather bag were spread out on a bench. Selby studied them carefully. The briefcase had held a new pad of yellow, legal-size foolscap and two pencils. The bag had held three suits of underwear, one clean pair of pyjamas, some new socks, two shirts, shaving things, hairbrush, comb, clean handkerchiefs freshly folded, and a pair of Pullman slippers.

'Laundry marks?' Selby asked.

'Not a one,' Perkins said. 'Some of the things are new. The others, such as the handkerchiefs, haven't even a laundry mark. That means he must have lived at home and his wife had a laundress.'

Selby looked at the briefcase. On the inside of the flap had been stencilled in gold: FRED ALBION ROFF.

'Where do you suppose he slept last night?' Selby asked.

Perkins raised his brows. 'I don't get it. What does that have to do with it?'

43

Selby said, 'His pyjamas are clean, freshly ironed. Everything in the bag is clean. Unless he sent out some laundry, he must have started from his home this morning, with his bag all packed for a stay of several days.'

'He's supposed to live in Los Angeles,' Perkins said, 'but there's no label on the inside of his suit.'

'Let's take a look at the left front tail of those shirts.'

'Why?'

'Sometimes the figures there tell a lot. The size of the shirt is stamped there, also some figures that frequently give a clue as to the place where the shirt was sold.'

They unfolded the shirts. There was a series of cabalistic numbers stamped in indelible black ink. 'I think a haberdasher can tell you something about those,' Selby said. 'Perhaps the shipment of shirts can be traced from the factory. What was in his pockets?'

'Thirty or forty dollars, a handkerchief, clean; a watch, knife, fountain pen, and a leather key container with half a dozen keys.'

'No cards?'

'Not a thing.'

'The handkerchief's clean?'

'Just like you find it there.'

Selby regarded the briefcase thoughtfully. 'Looks rather well used.'

'Does for a fact,' Perkins agreed.

'Yet it hasn't been scuffed up much, and it's held its shape – strange thing that *everything* he had was clean. Don't suppose he sent out any laundry?'

'The hotel says not. He registered, ordered breakfast, and croaked.'

'And everything the man had was clean, not a soiled garment in the outfit. It's a good-sized bag, Harry. How does all this stuff fit in it?'

'Room to spare.'

Selby pondered thoughtfully over the collection of objects on the coroner's counter. He picked up the briefcase, regarded the polished underside of the handle. 'If Los Angeles doesn't give you any clue, Harry, wire the State Bar Association and see if he's a lawyer.'

'What makes you think he's a lawyer, Doug?'

'The briefcase, the whole thing.'

'If he came from some place other than Los Angeles, where are the clothes he wore on the train?'

'I'll bite,' Selby said cheerfully. 'I'm just a bystander here, you know, Harry.'

The coroner tried a pun. 'Well, he sure as heck came *clean* from Los Angeles if he lived there.'

Selby left the coroner grinning at his own joke.

CHAPTER SEVEN

On the way uptown from Harry Perkins' office, Selby stopped in at the hotel, where he found Frank Norwalk behind the desk, going about his duties in dour silence.

'You don't seem very cheerful,' Selby said.

'You wouldn't either, if every time a man dropped dead of heart failure someone tried to make it appear you had a hotel full of murderers.'

'It wasn't heart failure.'

'Well, suicide, then.'

Selby smiled and shook his head.

'That's the worst of running a hotel,' Norwalk said. 'Some man comes in and pays you five bucks for a room with a bath and does you five thousand dollars' worth of damage by getting bumped off. What have you found out, anything?'

Selby cheerfully washed his hands of all responsibility. 'I understand Carl Gifford is getting a statement from the room steward who took the breakfast up.'

Norwalk thought that over for a moment, started to say something, then checked himself.

'What is it?' Selby asked.

Norwalk said, 'I hate to tell you fellows anything because you always go out and magnify it and distort it and make a mystery out of it and then the newspapers play it up big, but – say, how soon do you think that man died after he drank the coffee?'

'Almost instantly,' Selby said. 'I think when the sheriff fingerprints the metal dish covers that were over the food he'll find they hadn't even been lifted. The man probably poured himself a cup of coffee first thing, took a good big drink of it and was dead within a matter of seconds. That poison can act very rapidly.'

'He checked in at eight-thirty. The room service records show that the order for breakfast came in a little after nine, about nine-ten or nine-fifteen.'

Selby nodded.

Norwalk said, 'One of the tenants here in the building happened to notice a woman coming out of that room about quarter of ten.'

'Out of *that* room?'

'That's right.'

'He's certain?'

'Claims he is.'

'Who is he?'

'Coleman Dexter. Has a room on the sixth floor, been here for a month or six weeks. Has some money to invest in an orange grove, but wants to get just the right property before he buys. Been looking around a bit. Pretty smart individual. Not the type you'd think would make a mistake.'

'How did he happen to notice this woman?' Selby asked.

'He just happened to be in the hallway. She had an armful of laundry.'

'Where is he?'

'In six-forty-two. You want him?'

Without pausing to remember that he no longer had any official status in Madison County, Selby nodded. 'That woman may be very, very important, Frank.'

'Well … Oh, I suppose so. I guess we're in a mess and we've got to see it through. Want to go up, or want to have him come down?'

'He's in his room now?'

'He was a few minutes ago. I think he still is.'

Norwalk nodded to the girl at the switchboard and said, 'Give Coleman Dexter a ring in six-forty-two.'

'We may as well go up,' Selby said.

The girl at the switchboard caught Selby's words, plugged in a line, pushed a button, said, 'Good afternoon, Mr Dexter. Mr Norwalk wishes to know if it would be all right if he came up … yes … right away … yes, thank you.' She nodded and said, 'He's expecting you.'

Norwalk walked around from behind the counter, went to the elevator and rode to the sixth floor in silence. They walked down the long corridor, turned to the right and paused before a door at the far end of the corridor. Norwalk knocked.

Dexter, a jovial, heavy-set man, jerked the door open, said, 'Come on in, Frank. I don't know as …'

He broke off as he saw Selby.

'Major Selby,' Norwalk introduced. Then, looking over at the table asked, 'What are you doing, still studying maps?'

Dexter gripped Selby's hand. 'Pleased to meet you, Major,' and then, turning to Norwalk, said, 'still studying maps. Don't mind telling you, though, that I've just about made up my mind to close a deal. However, I'm going at it pretty cautiously, looking at the temperature records for the past twenty-five years, studying rainfall and soil maps. When I buy anything, I like to take lots of time doing it.'

Norwalk said, 'Selby was formerly district attorney here.'

'I see,' Dexter said vaguely.

'We were interested in the woman you saw coming out of six-nineteen.'

Dexter nodded.

'Can you,' Selby asked, 'fix the time?'

'I can fix the time right down to the split second, Major,' Dexter said, but added somewhat ruefully, 'I'm not so certain of my description of the woman.'

'Suppose you run over it again for us,' Norwalk said.

'Well, I slept rather late this morning. I got up around quarter to nine, had a shower, a shave, and went out to get some breakfast. I came back at exactly nine-fifty and the elevator boy took me up to the sixth floor. I was smoking and the cigarette had just about got down to the point of diminishing returns. I took a last drag at it, and ground it out in that cylinder of sand that is just to the right of the elevators. And while I was doing that, the door of the room just behind me opened, and I vaguely realized someone was coming out. The door closed and this woman was walking toward me just as I straightened up. I don't think she'd seen me there by the elevator. She was looking down the corridor and she seemed to be just a little bit startled when I straightened up. I'd been rather motionless grinding out the cigarette stub. Well, she had some clothes over her arm, apparently a bundle of laundry. I wouldn't even have noticed her if it hadn't been for the way she jumped when she saw me.'

'Where did she go?' Selby asked.

'I haven't the faintest idea,' Dexter said.

'She didn't go down in the elevator?'

'No she didn't. She must have gone into one of the other rooms. But I didn't hear the door unlock. I have my own problems. I've been trying to find some suitable investment and it's been quite a job getting *just* what I wanted. I still don't know whether I have it, but I think I have. I'm going to take another look this afternoon and then make up my mind.'

'Can you describe her?'

49

'She was rather tall – not too tall, but rather tall. She wasn't fat and she wasn't old, perhaps around thirty, and good-looking. There was something incongruous about this laundry and the way she was dressed.'

'Blonde or brunette?'

'Brunette. I remember that. That is, I don't remember her hair but her eyes were large and quite dark. She was dressed in some sort of a dark dress, but whether it was – I just can't tell you, Major. Sometimes I think I can see her very plainly and then when I try to concentrate on something or other about her appearance, she begins to get vague to me and I know I'm just kidding myself. I'm terribly sorry I didn't pay more attention to her. The only thing I can tell you is that this bundle of laundry was done up in a man's shirt.'

'You're certain of the time?'

Dexter grinned. 'That's one thing I can give you – the time. It was exactly nine forty-nine. There's a clock in the lobby that's regulated by Western Union time and I checked my watch with it. I was three minutes fast and decided that that was just a little too fast so I set my watch back three minutes in the elevator.'

'How about the elevator operator?' Selby asked Norwalk.

Norwalk shook his head. 'He remembers the time, all right. He took Dexter down to breakfast and then brought him back and it was right around nine-fifty, and he remembers Dexter setting his watch back in the elevator, but he didn't see the woman.'

Dexter said by way of explanation, 'The boy had closed the door and the elevator had gone down. I'd put my watch back in my pocket and was grinding out the cigarette stub. It must have been eight or ten seconds after the elevator went down. And now I'm thinking of it, I can remember something else. I can remember the door opened for a few seconds before she came out. I remember now that I heard the click of the door and then she came out and I straightened up and saw her sort of jump. She may have been looking around to see if the corridor was clear. Any chance she might have ... well, you know, had anything to do with *it*?'

Selby said, 'He must have been dead at least twenty minutes before she came out of the room. But I *am* interested in the fact that she was carrying some clothes with her. You didn't see where she went?'

'She was walking toward me when I saw her and I turned around and walked on down the corridor. She must have followed me for a while, but I don't know how far. And there's one more thing that ... well, I'm not at all certain of it, but now that I keep thinking back on it, she *may* have dropped a paper. It seems to me I remember seeing something white fluttering toward the floor. It was while I was bent over.'

'It could have been a piece of cloth, perhaps a handkerchief,' Selby said.

'No, more like a paper, a newspaper clipping or something – something that fluttered. Shucks, Major, you know how those things are. You've got your mind full of something and you have some casual experience, then you try to remember back and it's ... something like trying to recall a dream. You think you remember things but you can't be certain. Somehow I get the feeling there *may* have been a paper that dropped. I can't be certain of it. If I'd been certain of it, or if I'd even seen it clearly, I'd have begged her pardon and told her she'd dropped something. But I had my mind on this deal and I was absorbed thinking about ...'

The telephone rang.

Dexter said, 'Pardon me, I'm waiting for a call on this property. I've submitted a counter-offer.'

He crossed over to the telephone, said, 'Hello,' then after a moment asked, 'who ... who is it you want? ... Oh ... just a moment.' He swung around from the telephone, said to Selby, 'I beg your pardon, Major, but I guess you're *Doug* Selby, aren't you?'

'Yes.'

'The sheriff wants to speak with you.'

Selby walked over and picked up the telephone. 'Hello, Rex, what is it?'

Brandon said, 'Two things, Doug, and they bother me. I'd like to talk with you.'

'Can you tell me what they are over the telephone?'

'Sure.'

'Go ahead.'

'For one thing, this Henry Farley we've been questioning has a criminal record.'

'Oh, oh,' Selby said.

'And,' Brandon went on dryly, 'he was arrested again in Los Angeles about eight months ago on suspicion of larceny. Evidently he had quite a roll with him. Of course, he says he was innocent and all that, but you know how those things go.'

'Go ahead,' Selby said.

'The man who got him out – or as he expresses it, the man who "sprung" him was A B Carr.'

'Getting close to home,' Selby said dryly.

'And the other thing that bothers me, and it *really* bothers me,' the sheriff went on, 'is that Doctor Thurman just telephoned; said he heard that the man was poisoned because he drank some coffee that had come up with a breakfast order ...'

'Well,' Selby prompted as Brandon stopped talking.

'Well,' the sheriff blurted, 'Doc Thurman opened him up and took a look at his stomach first rattle out of the box. The man had had breakfast within an hour of the time he was killed, and it was a good substantial breakfast. As nearly as the Doc can tell, it was ham and eggs, toast, coffee, oatmeal, and stewed prunes.'

'Within an hour?' Selby asked.

'That's right.'

'I can't understand it,' Selby said. 'Why should he want *two* breakfasts?'

'I don't know.'

'How about Gifford, does he understand it?'

'Gifford isn't even trying to. That criminal record on the waiter is enough for him. He thinks he's got the murderer. I'd like to talk with you, Doug.'

'I'll be right over,' Selby said.

CHAPTER EIGHT

Doug Selby found Rex Brandon restlessly pacing the floor, something that was most unusual for the sheriff.

Brandon motioned Doug to a chair, indicated the ex-district attorney's old brier pipe, which the sheriff had once more taken out from his desk, and the humidor beside it.

'Sit down, Doug. Light up. Let's talk for a minute. If you don't mind.'

'Not a bit,' Selby said. 'I'd like it.'

'I'm perplexed about this whole thing,' Brandon said, 'and darned uneasy about it, Doug. Carl Gifford is going ahead like a house afire, but if anything happens and we get caught in a box canyon, I know just as well as I know anything that Gifford will pull out and leave me holding the sack. I don't like it.'

'What's this about the breakfast?' Selby asked.

'That's just it. The chap had breakfast just before he registered at the hotel. So far we haven't been able to find where he ate that breakfast, but Doc Thurman says there's no question about it.'

'Then why would he have ordered another breakfast?'

'That's just it. The question is *did* he order another breakfast?'

'You mean someone else ordered it for him?' Selby asked.

'Exactly.'

'You mean someone else in the hotel could simply pick up the telephone and say, "This is room six-nineteen and I want breakfast sent up"?'

'Well,' Brandon said, 'that's what I was getting at, but, of course, there's another possible solution. This Henry Farley takes the orders for breakfast when he's there. Then he goes out and delivers them. He doesn't go back to pick up the dishes until the slack time in the morning around eleven o'clock. If the maid makes up the rooms before that, she puts the table and the dishes out in the corridor and they wait there until Farley picks them up.'

'Then this chap Farley could have made up the whole business?' Selby asked. 'Simply pretended he'd received an order from six-nineteen and started up there with the tray?'

'That's what Gifford thinks.'

'But if he'd done that,' Selby pointed out, 'the minute he knocked at the door of the room, this man, Roff, would have said, "Look here, my man, you've got the wrong room. I didn't order any breakfast." And that would also have been the case if someone else had phoned in the order and given the wrong room number.'

'Exactly,' the sheriff said dryly, 'but that's Gifford's idea. He thinks that the waiter said there'd been some mistake and put the tray down and went off to investigate and Roff decided he'd like to have another cup of coffee and went over and helped himself.'

'That's absolutely absurd,' Selby said.

'I know it is.'

Selby said, 'If you were in a room in a hotel and hadn't ordered breakfast, and a waiter came up with a table and a tray, you'd tell him there'd been a mistake. You might let him use the telephone, but you wouldn't want him to bring the breakfast into the room and then go away and leave it, and he certainly wouldn't want to.'

Brandon nodded.

'Just what does Farley say? What does he claim happened?'

'That's just it,' the sheriff said dryly. 'When we questioned Farley, instead of going at him diplomatically, Gifford started riding him roughshod and started right in on the man's past – asking him how long he'd been in Madison City, where he came from, whether he'd been in any trouble before and things of that sort. Then it came out that the man had been convicted of minor crimes – that he'd been in trouble for boot-legging during the prohibition era, and had been mixed up in some race track stuff.'

'Then what happened?' Selby asked.

'Then Gifford just about as good as accused Farley of either murdering this man, Roff, or standing in cahoots with the murderer.'

'And what happened?'

'Farley dried up like a clam. He simply sat there and smiled and said, "Gentlemen, I think I'll telephone my lawyer if you don't mind." '

'Then what?'

'Gifford said he could telephone his lawyer afterwards. He wanted him to answer a few questions first.'

'And what did Farley do?'

'Simply smiled at him.'

'What finally happened?'

'He telephoned his lawyer.'

'Then what?'

'His lawyer is closeted with him now.'

'And the lawyer?'

'Alfonse Baker Carr,' the sheriff said disgustedly. 'Leave it to all these city crooks. The minute they get into a jam they simply pick up a telephone and yell for old A B C.'

'I'm rather surprised that Carr would have taken his case,' Selby said.

'Why not? In view of what we know ...'

'I know, but Carr couldn't have known all the ramifications when Farley telephoned him.'

'Well, he knows them now,' the sheriff said dryly. 'He ...'

A knock sounded on the door of Brandon's private office. A moment later a deputy opened it and said, 'Mr A B Carr would like to talk with you, Sheriff.'

'There you are,' the sheriff said.

Selby smiled. 'Well, let's see what *he* has to say, Rex.'

'Show him in,' the sheriff said.

A B Carr was never more gravely courteous.

'Good afternoon, gentlemen. I'm glad that you're here, Major. I certainly feel that I owe you an apology, Sheriff.'

Brandon made an inarticulate grunt.

'I take it,' Carr said, smiling disarmingly, 'that there's no objection to talking frankly in front of Major Selby?'

Brandon silently indicated a chair.

Carr settled himself in the chair, managing to invest himself as he did so with the manner of a distinguished guest. 'My client,' he said, 'my poor unfortunate client. My ignorant, obstinate, thickheaded client. My dumb, mulish fool of a client!'

'Farley?' the sheriff asked.

'Farley,' Carr said in his rich, resonant voice that would have been the envy of any actor on the stage. 'Of course,' he went on, 'you can't blame the poor man in one way. He's the product of the cities and the slums, gentlemen, he's accustomed to the roughshod methods of the city police – and I take it that you won't think the comment is disparaging in any way if I say that the manner of your new district attorney was such that it brought back an association of ideas. A certain fear of the police third-degree of – well, gentlemen, there's no reason why I shouldn't say it plainly – of the frame-up.'

Brandon, always irritated by Carr's manner, resentful of his magnetic personality and richly resonant voice, merely settled down in a chair and waited for the criminal lawyer to proceed.

Selby, frankly enjoying the show A B C was putting on, said, smilingly, 'Well, of course, Carr, when a waiter who has delivered a poisoned breakfast to a man in a hotel refuses to discuss the matter, there's always *some* ground for suspicion.'

'Exactly,' Carr said. 'Your point is exceptionally well taken, Major, but if you'll pardon me, may I point out that his refusal to make a frank statement came *after* the somewhat belligerent attitude on the part of the district attorney, not, as your comment seems to imply, that the attitude of the district attorney was the result of …'

'Never mind stalling around,' Brandon said. 'What's the story?'

'Quite right, quite right,' Carr said, beaming at the irate sheriff. 'After all, gentlemen, you're busy men. We're all busy men. You want to get right down to the meat in the nutshell. But please, gentlemen, let me first apologize for the attitude of my client and endeavour to explain it. It was unfortunate. I have told him that it was most unfortunate. He should have made a frank statement. He has sought to justify his position with me by explaining that in view of the attitude of your district attorney he felt certain there was going to be an attempt to frame him for murder on account of his past record, a record with which I am fully familiar, gentlemen, and which comprises only offences of a relatively minor nature.'

'What does he say?' Brandon asked.

Carr nodded gravely. 'He says that he received an order for breakfast, to be delivered to room six-nineteen, that he took it to room six-nineteen and found the door locked. He knocked on the door – a rather perfunctory knock such as waiters give on occasions.'

'Go on,' Brandon said as Carr stopped talking to look at the two men, as though making certain that they had a complete grasp of the situation up to that point.

'Then,' Carr went on, 'the door was opened. This man had evidently been unpacking his bag, getting some laundry ready to be sent out. The waiter remembers there was a pile of soiled clothes on the bed, that the man was lightly flushed, as though he had just straightened up. He said, "Oh, it's the breakfast," or something to that effect, and then said, "Put it anywhere," and turned back to the clothes on the bed as though he had no further interest in the breakfast.

'My client arranged the tray and rather hung around for a moment, expecting that he would receive a tip, but the tenant of the room dismissed him with a curt "That's all," and that's every single thing my client knows, gentlemen.'

'There's no question of identity?' Selby asked. 'It was the same man?'

'Unquestionably. The dead man seems to have had a distinctive appearance, and my client identifies him positively.'

'There wasn't any woman in the room?'

'No, the man was alone, save, of course, that my client didn't look in the closet or bathroom. The man seemed rather brusque, perhaps a trifle put out about something. Aside from that, there was nothing unusual about the entire affair. It differed in no way from hundreds of other room-service orders.'

Selby glanced at the sheriff, said abruptly to Carr, 'What's *your* idea?'

Carr's face was utterly guileless. 'Gentlemen, I haven't any idea, because I don't know enough about the facts of the case. I understand generally, the man was found dead in that room and that there is some contention that the coffee had been poisoned. I think that Henry Farley is the victim of circumstances. He has a record of several minor crimes, and a peculiar coincidence has sucked him into the vortex of events having to do with murder. But, nevertheless, he should have told his story fully and frankly. He has nothing to conceal. I am willing to admit that I have rebuked him for the attitude he adopted. But that, gentlemen, is all water under the bridge.

'Gentlemen, I haven't any definite theory, but, of course, the human mind may always speculate, and the mind that has had some experience with murders is prone to do so. All I can do now is to speculate. I believe my client. I have known him for some time. His mind is perhaps somewhat warped in its sense of right and wrong, but he is in some ways an admirable client. He tells his lawyer the absolute truth. In fact, gentlemen, you will sometimes find that this most commendable trait is more developed in the underprivileged who have been accused of crime than in the more fortunate persons who so frequently try to deceive their own counsel.

'Of course, the laundry on the bed is a significant item. Remember also that the doors of the hotel have no spring locks. I do feel almost certain that the man went on with the checking of his laundry, that for some reason he stepped out of his room. Perhaps – and this certainly isn't beyond the bounds of reasonable conjecture – he was deliberately lured out of the room, decoyed by some message, something that had been deliberately planned.

'Then you can realize what happened, gentlemen. I need not even bother to point it out. The fleeting shadow, slipping out through the door of an adjoining room, gliding furtively into the room where the breakfast lay so invitingly on the tray. The swift motion of a hand containing a medicine dropper. For the moment the acrid odour of the poison. Then the sugar cubes absorb their deadly potion and remain innocently white on the tray. The murderer backs slowly away. His work is done, well done. He darts out of the room and back into the adjoining room from whence he had come.

'Then after a few moments the victim returns. Whatever had been on his mind now troubles him no longer. He is tired from a long journey, perhaps on a crowded bus, perhaps on an equally crowded train. He is hungry. He draws a chair up to the table with its snowy linen and its tempting array of dishes. He pours out steaming amber coffee. He adds thick cream, the sort of cream, gentlemen, that one is able to find only in a rural community, in the midst of a rich dairying country. And then, gentlemen …'

Carr paused dramatically, reached one of his hands out as though picking up lumps of sugar, '… then he picks up the sugar. One lump. Two lumps.' Carr's fingers went through all the motions of picking up the sugar lumps, conveying them to a cup of coffee, dropping them in. 'And he stirs the coffee with a teaspoon, thinking perhaps of his business, totally unaware of the deadly potion that he holds in his hand.'

Carr stopped for a moment.

Brandon started to say something, moved impatiently.

Selby checked him with a glance.

'By this time,' Carr went on in his smooth resonant voice, 'the coffee has become cool enough so that it can be imbibed in deep gulps. You will notice the importance of that, gentlemen, because it not only coincides with the facts, but bears out the theory I have advanced. The fact that the coffee has stood long enough to become slightly cool is a necessary precedent to the murder. The stage is all set. The victim holds the coffee cup in his hands. He takes three or four deep gulps before he suddenly notices a peculiar aroma, a rather unpleasant taste. He puts the coffee cup back on the saucer, reaches for his napkin, starts to get up out of his chair, and falls over on his face. There is a convulsion, a pathetic last-minute attempt to crawl to the telephone, then a shudder and the man lies still in death, leaving the murderer to check out of the hotel and mingle with the stream of the travelling public, an unidentified bit of human flotsam.

'I have, perhaps, enlarged somewhat on the dramatic aspect of the case, gentlemen, because it seems to me to be almost the perfect crime. Certainly a most puzzling crime, one that compels my interest because of the very interesting possibilities it presents and baffling circumstances with which you must find yourselves confronted.'

The sheriff said, 'That's all right, but you just overlooked one thing. The man didn't reach for that breakfast in a hurry because he ...'

Selby interrupted hastily, 'I take it, Carr, that you've remonstrated with Farley for his attitude in the matter.'

'Indeed I have. The man has nothing to conceal. He should have told his story frankly. I am only too well aware, Major, that this initial reticence is merely another black mark on the record against him. But I can assure you that the man has absolutely convinced me of his complete innocence.'

'You're going to represent him?'

Carr's eyebrows raised in astonished incredulity. 'Surely, Major, he's not going to be charged with anything!'

'If he is charged, you're going to represent him?'

'Well now,' Carr said, 'that of course is looking rather far ahead, but I would say offhand that my answer would be in the affirmative. I am interested in justice. I am particularly interested in protecting the underdog. And here is a man who seems peculiarly entitled to such protection as I can give, a man who has had perhaps an unfortunate record but who is working diligently in an attempt at social rehabilitation. Yes, gentlemen, if he is charged with anything, you may take it for granted that I will represent him.'

'All right, that's all,' Brandon said angrily. 'Is he going to give us a statement now?'

'I certainly see no reason why he shouldn't. I should suggest that as a matter of courtesy it might be well for me to be present when the statement is given, I am to act as the man's lawyer in the event he *should* be charged with anything.'

Selby said, 'We can take that up later, but in the meantime, Carr, there's something the sheriff wanted to ask you about.'

Brandon gave Selby a quizzical glance, as though trying to read his friend's mind.

'Why, certainly,' Carr said with easy affability. 'I am certainly at your service.'

'I don't know how much you know about the circumstances surrounding the finding of the body,' Selby said.

'Hardly a thing,' Carr replied. 'The first I had heard of it was when Farley summoned me to the county jail, and that which he told me was just the information that had been picked up by the employees there at the hotel, a certain amount of backstairs gossip, you know, gentlemen.'

Selby nodded.

'Apparently, shortly after he had entered the room, this man who registered under the name of Roff called up one of the florists and asked to have a white gardenia sent to him.'

'Indeed,' Carr said, and his face was as a wooden mask.

Selby kept his eyes fixed on Carr's. 'I happened to notice this morning that you were at the train when I came in.'

'I didn't see you,' Carr said. 'Of course, I hardly expected to see you, and then in your uniform ... one sees so many uniforms these days.'

'Never mind that,' Selby interrupted, 'but the point is that *you* were wearing a white gardenia.'

'I was,' Carr said. 'I was indeed.'

'And that you met two other people who were wearing white gardenias.'

For a moment Carr seemed completely puzzled, then suddenly he threw back his head and laughed with every semblance of genuine, wholehearted enjoyment.

It wasn't until he caught the look in Selby's eyes and saw the glowering suspicion of Brandon's countenance that Carr abruptly ceased laughing.

'You'll pardon me, gentlemen. I certainly trust you'll pardon me. I didn't want to appear impolite, but the humour of the situation thrust itself forcibly upon me. Here I have been commiserating with my client because of an unfortunate combination of coincidences, and now I myself seem to have become the victim of just such a series of coincidences.'

'Not at all,' Selby said as suavely as old A B C himself. 'I was merely suggesting that under the circumstances you might care to give us something of an explanation, in view of the fact that you have rebuked your client for *his* refusal to co-operate with the authorities in their investigation.'

'A neat point,' Carr said, nodding approvingly. 'Very neatly expressed, Major.'

'Well, go ahead. Tell us,' Brandon blurted.

'And that,' Carr went on without even turning to look at the irate sheriff, 'would account for the persistent inquiries of that very charming newspaper reporter, Miss Sylvia Martin, who was apparently getting ready to ask me a somewhat similar question when the ringing of the telephone interrupted our conference – the telephone call, of course, being the summons of Henry Farley to come at once to the jail on a matter of the greatest importance.'

'You still haven't answered the question,' Brandon said.

'The answer to that question is quite simple,' Carr replied, turning now to look at the sheriff and moving his hands in a gesture that seemed to bare his very soul to the scrutiny of the county official.

'I am engaged in a case involving the contest of a will in an estate involving perhaps a million dollars. The case goes on trial tomorrow before a jury, and naturally there are certain last-minute preparations. Strange as it may seem, my negotiations have been through a third party, my only contact with my client by mail. So you see, my client, whom I'd never met, was to have joined me today for a conference. She talked with me over the long-distance telephone day before yesterday and wanted to know how she could make herself known to me. I have no office here, and since I am a bachelor, she hardly cared to drive directly to my house – well, I suggested that she might wear a white gardenia and that I too would wear a white gardenia. I believe you saw me at my conference in the restaurant. In fact, that conference seems to have aroused the interest of Miss Sylvia Martin.'

'It still doesn't account for the two *other* people you picked up at the train,' Selby said.

'That is the interesting part of it, Major. I went to the train, expecting to meet this client. I see no reason why I should be at all reticent concerning her identity. She is Miss Anita Eldon, the daughter of Martha Otley.'

'Go ahead,' Brandon said gruffly.

'Well, Miss Eldon neglected to tell me by what means she would arrive. She said that she would be here this morning, and that I should meet her at the depot. Rather foolishly, I failed to take into consideration the fact that she meant the bus depot. I went down to the railroad depot to meet the only train which arrived in the morning. There I saw a woman wearing a white gardenia. I knew that she could hardly have been the person I expected, but I thought perhaps Miss Eldon had been detained and had sent this person with some message. So I introduced

65

myself, and asked this woman if she had a message for me. She nodded and said she did. And then, as I was escorting her to my automobile, I found there was still another person, this time a man, wearing a white gardenia, who seemed to attach himself to us as though he really belonged. I thought at the moment he was travelling with the woman who had the message for me, so I took them both in my automobile and drove them uptown. It wasn't until they were ensconced in the car that it turned out they had no message for me, but were merely expecting to meet someone who would be at the train to receive them. Under the circumstances, I hardly knew what to do. Suddenly it occurred to me that my own client had meant she would fly to Los Angeles and then come here by bus and so be at the bus depot. So I went to the bus depot and parked my car, went inside and made interrogations, and, sure enough, learned that a person who answered the description of the party I was expecting had waited for about five minutes, then had impatiently announced she was going out to get something to eat. I think that you gentlemen saw this woman and realize she is hardly the type who would wait very long for anyone.'

'Go on,' Brandon said somewhat wearily. 'It's a good story. We'll hear all of it while we're about it.'

'But that's all there is to it,' Carr assured him. 'When I returned to my automobile, I found that my two passengers had departed. Undoubtedly they had compared notes, realized that I wasn't the gentleman that they expected to meet and had gone on about their own business.'

'So,' Selby said, smiling, 'I take it you looked in the principal restaurants, found your party sitting there, eating, introduced yourself to her, apologized and joined her.'

'Exactly,' Carr said, 'and expressed very succinctly, Major.'

Selby glanced at Brandon.

'I guess that's all,' the sheriff said wearily.

'Thank you,' Carr said, 'and once more let me apologize for the attitude of Mr Farley and explain to you just what caused his reticence.'

Brandon said nothing.

Selby bowed Carr out of the office, his manner matching that of the adroit criminal lawyer. 'I think,' Selby said, 'we understand your position thoroughly.'

'Thank you, Major. Thank you very much.'

Selby closed the door, turned back to Brandon.

Brandon made a grimace, said, 'There you are. That story isn't Farley's story, it's Carr's story. Farley summoned Carr. He told Carr just what the situation was, and it took Carr just about ten seconds to think up the best way of presenting a yarn that …'

'I don't know,' Selby said. 'I'm not so certain that story isn't the truth. I'd better tell you what I've found out.'

'What?'

Selby told Brandon of his interview with Coleman Dexter, and the sheriff listened attentively, rolling himself a cigarette in typical cowpuncher manner as he listened, then closing the sack by catching the drawstring in his teeth, finishing with his cigarette and snapping a match into flame with a single motion of his capable thumb.

'Humph!' he said when Selby had finished.

'Now then,' Selby went on, 'Dexter thinks there was a paper that fell out from under the woman's arm. You can see what that means, Rex. She had gone through the man's briefcase. She had taken out his papers, and in order to cover that theft, she had taken the soiled clothes from the man's bed and placed the papers in them – making it appear she was a maid leaving the room with some laundry.'

'And she dropped one paper?' Brandon said. 'Did she stoop to pick it up?'

'Dexter doesn't know. He doesn't even know that she dropped one.'

'Suppose she did. Then what became of the paper?' Brandon asked.

'Norwalk is checking, trying to find out. But it occurs to me, Rex, the papers that were in the man's briefcase may have been the motive for the murder. The entire thing was staged in an attempt to get possession of those papers and to seal the man's lips.'

'Well, we don't seem to be getting anywhere with motive,' Brandon said.

Selby said, 'The name Fred Albion Roff is the man's name. It's stamped on the inside of his briefcase. My best guess is the man's a lawyer.'

'What gives you that impression?'

'Quite a few things. I think he's a country lawyer. There are no laundry marks on his clothes. In some of the country towns in the Midwest it's possible to get a laundress regularly. In the cities, or out here on the coast, you just can't get help now, not regularly. And as for his having been a lawyer, his briefcase is legal size. It's seen considerable use.'

'He might have been a salesman.'

'A salesman usually carries more papers,' Selby pointed out. 'He needs a price book, book of blank orders. He carries some correspondence. He carries some descriptive literature. Notice a salesman's briefcase and you'll nearly always find that it's pretty well pushed out of shape, bulging with a variegated assortment of material, thrown around in an automobile, badly scuffed up. This briefcase is old and worn but it has still retained its shape. It's a briefcase in which a lawyer might carry papers from his office to the courthouse; from his hotel in the State Capitol to the Supreme Court. It ...'

The telephone rang.

Brandon picked up the receiver, said, 'Hello ... yes, this is Brandon speaking ... all right, Norwalk, what have you found?'

The sheriff listened for a few seconds, then said, 'Okay, we'll be down.'

He turned to Selby, dropped the receiver into place.

'One of the bellboys found a sheet of legal paper with some typewriting on it lying on the carpet in the corridor of the sixth floor of the hotel. He picked up the paper, saw that it seemed to be part of a legal document, took it down to the office and left it with the telephone operator telling her that if anyone missed it he'd found it on the sixth floor. Norwalk has just found out about it.'

'What sort of a document?' Selby asked.

'Norwalk says it's apparently a typewritten legal argument of some sort.'

'There's no name on the paper? Nothing printed at the bottom?' Selby asked excitedly. 'Sometimes lawyers have their name and address printed on each sheet of legal paper they use.'

'Not a thing, just plain legal paper. Let's go take a look at it.'

Chapter Nine

Over at the hotel, Selby and Rex Brandon pondered over the single sheet of typewritten paper which Norwalk had produced.

It was a page which bore at the bottom the figure '-7-' and was quite evidently a part of a manuscript which had consisted of a number of pages.

'It's part of a lawyer's brief,' Selby reported after he had read it through. 'It involves a question of adverse possession of real property where there has been a tenancy in common. That's rather a complicated legal question and, as nearly as one can gather, the man who wrote this brief – whoever he may have been – was trying to establish that after there had been a definite disclaimer of the co-tenancy relation on the part of one of the purported co-tenants, and thereafter a claim established to the entire property, there could be an adverse possession as against the other co-tenant, but it's hard to tell just what position … Rex, let's play a hunch.'

'What?'

Selby said, 'I have an idea this murder may well have been connected with the will contest case that's going on trial tomorrow. Inez Stapleton, who is representing the contestant, tells me that one of the contestants resides in Kansas, and that death of the decedent occurred in Kansas. Let's wire the Secretary of the State Bar Association of Kansas and find out if they have a Fred Albion Roff listed as an attorney, and where he's located.'

Brandon thought for a moment, then moved over to a desk in Norwalk's office and pulled a telegraph blank toward him.

'Doug,' he said as he pulled a pencil from his pocket, 'I wish I had you working with me on this case.'

Selby grinned. 'You've got me.'

Less than two hours later, Sheriff Brandon had an answer to his wire:

FRED ALBION ROFF ATTORNEY AT LAW WITH OFFICE AT EMPALA KANSAS BEEN PRACTISING THAT COMMUNITY MORE THAN THIRTY YEARS ACTIVE IN POLITICS AND HAS SOME LOCAL REPUTATION AS AN ORATOR OF CONSIDERABLE ABILITY IN ADDITION HIS LAW PRACTICE REPORTED TO MAKE CONS1DERABLE INCOME BUYING AND SELLING REAL PROPERTY.

CHAPTER TEN

Late that afternoon, Selby entered Inez Stapleton's office just in time to encounter a big-boned, heavily fleshed man going out.

The man gave Selby the benefit of a quick appraisal which somehow seemed to cover only the superficialities. It was as though the man felt sufficiently smug in the security of his own position to see only the things in life and in people that he wanted to see.

Selby walked through the reception room and saw Inez Stapleton seated at her desk, very apparently greatly discouraged.

'Is it that bad, Inez?' Selby asked.

She gave him a wan smile, said nothing.

With the assurance of an old friend, Selby settled himself in the chair, and tamped tobacco into the familiar old brier pipe which he had rescued from the sheriff's office. 'Want to talk about it?' he asked.

Inez pointed her finger in a jabbing gesture at the door through which the big man had just departed and said, 'That is W Barclay Stanton.'

'Your associate?' Selby asked.

'My associate,' she said acidly. 'The man who is representing Hervey Preston, the brother, a small-town politician, a spellbinder of the old school. In his own bailiwick he's doubtless deadly in front of a jury, but he's come to Madison City, making no concessions to the fact that he's a stranger here, and that in this court he is without following or influence. He has carried with him all of the stuffed-shirt arrogance that goes with his particular type.'

'You mean he'll want to take an important part in the trial of the case and crowd you in the background?'

'Not that exactly. Gosh, Doug, I wouldn't care if he pushed me clean out of the courtroom, if he could win the case. But what I mean is that he's the typical stuffed shirt. He's lived long enough in one place and that place has been small enough so that whenever he says anything, the newspapers play it up. They can't have a political banquet without having him as the keynoter. He is the big shot in the Chamber of Commerce, a director in a bank. When he stands up in front of a jury in his own home town, the jurors are impressed with his prestige and he's impressed with his own prestige, and the combination makes for a certain amount of success.'

'Well, then he probably has something on the ball,' Selby said, his eyes twinkling in a reassuring smile through the first clouds of his pipe smoke.

'He probably did once,' Inez conceded, 'but as I size him up, for the last fifteen or twenty years he's been coasting along on that reputation. He's created a smug little niche for himself and hasn't kept pace with the times. He hasn't grown except around the waistband. He talks with all the old clichés of fifteen years ago. He's convinced he's a great orator. And he hasn't the faintest conception of the law in regard to will-contest cases.'

Selby said, 'Oh, well, kid him along, Inez. If he wants to get up in front, let him lead the shock troops and then after old A B Carr has punctured him, you can bring up the heavy reserves.'

She shook her head and said, 'You're just trying to reassure me, Doug. You know as well as I do that A B Carr will size him up at a glance and he'll be too shrewd to puncture him entirely out of the running. He'll leave him just enough pressure to keep going, egging the old boy along and giving him just enough encouragement so W Barclay Stanton will carry himself to his own *reductio ad absurdum*. Then, at the last minute, in front of the jury, with all of that deft skill that he has, A B Carr will strip aside the smug mask and show the jury that Stanton doesn't know what he's talking about, but that that hasn't kept him from talking about it at great length. He'll completely deflate him and leave the old stuffed shirt running on the rim,' and Inez smiled at her own mixed metaphor.

'Oh, it won't be that bad,' Selby said, laughing.

'The heck it won't,' she said bitterly, 'W Barclay Stanton is just the type to stand up in front of the jury and take fifteen or twenty minutes pouring fulsome praise on the jurors, telling them how pleased he is that the case is being tried before a body of men and women of such exceptional intelligence; that the parties are to be congratulated; that the jurors in this particular case are so intellectually superior to the average man and woman … Oh, nuts!'

Selby laughed. 'It's evidently been a bad day.'

'It has for a fact. My witnesses are melting like ice cubes left too long on the kitchen sink.'

'They always do that. They'll stiffen up in court.'

'Not with old A B Carr on the other side, they won't, Doug. Good heavens, some of those witnesses were so absolutely positive of things that sounded perfectly swell when they related them to me the first time. Little things that would show that bit-by-bit Martha Otley was carrying on a steady campaign to poison the mind of Eleanor Preston. And now they're getting just a little bit vague. When I start cross-examining them they begin to weaken and …'

'You've been working too hard,' Selby said, 'and you're taking the case too seriously. There are always breaks that you get from the other side. I've seen one of them today.'

'What do you mean, Doug?'

'Well, for instance let's consider the main character on the other side.'

'Who?'

'Anita Eldon.'

'What about her, Doug?'

Selby laughed and said, 'Wait until a Madison City jury takes a look at that gal.'

Inez Stapleton leaned forward to rest her elbow on the desk. 'What about her, Doug?'

'She's a hothouse flower.'

'Loud?'

'No not loud, just cultivated too much.'

'How do you mean, Doug?'

Selby said, 'I can't remember the exact words, but Sylvia Martin really covered it by saying that the woman put in as much care on her body as the average woman does on running a household, putting up preserves, cooking for her husband, washing dishes, getting the children off to school, darning their socks and all the rest of the things that go with running a household.'

Inez Stapleton's face became as a mask at the mention of Sylvia Martin. Selby, not noticing the danger signal, went on talking.

'You know, Inez, the more you think of it, the more you realize that that would be a good line to hand out to the jury. The hothouse flower type, the ... the orchid woman.'

Inez said very coldly, 'Thanks, Doug, it's an excellent suggestion, but I think I'd prefer to try the case without depending on Sylvia's descriptions.'

75

'Why, Inez? My gosh, you can't hit it off any better than that. Sylvia has been in the newspaper business, and …'

Selby broke off as he heard the front door open and close, saw Inez Stapleton's eyes raise and look past him over his shoulder.

Selby turned.

The woman who was standing in the doorway was a motherly type, with competent strength radiating from her as warmth radiates from a stove. Here was a woman who had gone through life, doing the things which life demanded, and, as her muscles had built up into strength and the slim lines of youth had vanished, she had gained in strength and in understanding, until now, beneath the aura of white hair, her features showed the calm confidence which comes from inner harmony.

She took one look at Inez Stapleton, then said, 'Now I just thought I'd find you here working on this case. You've been here altogether too long. You need some hot tea and a hot bath and a good dinner.'

She glanced somewhat curiously at Doug Selby, then said, 'Hope I'm not interrupting, but I just made up my mind I'd see this girl had something hot to eat.'

Inez Stapleton performed a brief introduction. 'Mrs Honcutt, Major Selby. Mrs Honcutt is the heir I'm representing, Doug.'

Selby, on his feet, was meeting the appraisal of sharp grey eyes that missed no detail.

'How de do,' Mrs Honcutt said, extending her hand.

'Major Selby,' Inez went on as Doug Selby was acknowledging the introduction, 'is a former district attorney here. He has an enviable record as a trial lawyer. He's back on a brief furlough and I've been sort of talking things over with him.'

'Well now,' Mrs Honcutt said, 'that just goes to show how I blunder into things. I should have known that you'd have a dinner date.'

Inez said somewhat wearily, 'Oh, but I haven't. Doug had just dropped in to pass the time of day. This is his first evening in town and he's all dated up.'

Mrs Honcutt frowned.

'Anyway,' Inez went on hastily, 'I really haven't any time for dinner. I've got to go over the notes I've made on the testimony of these witnesses and ...'

'That's exactly what I was afraid of,' Mrs Honcutt said. 'You'll work yourself to death on this thing. You've been here all day and you were here last night. From my room over there in the hotel I can look across and see your light, and it was still on when I went to bed, and I sat up until after nine o'clock, too.'

Inez smiled somewhat wearily. 'It was on long after that, Mrs Honcutt.'

'And I s'pose you were on the job again early this morning. Now you're going to come with me. I've got some things I want to talk to you about.'

'You're staying over at the Madison Hotel?' Selby asked.

'Yes. I'm in six-twenty-one. You know, a man dropped dead in the room next to me this morning.'

'So I understand,' Selby said. 'A lawyer, I believe, from somewhere in Kansas. You're from Kansas too, aren't you?'

'That's right. I'm from McKeesville. You say this man is from Kansas?'

'From Empalma, I understand.'

'Do tell,' Barbara Honcutt said. 'Empalma ain't so far from where we live. Not the way you measure distances out here. Of course, at home, we think it's quite a ways. What's his name?'

'Fred Albion Roff.'

'Never heard of him.'

Selby said, 'I was wondering if perhaps he might have had some connection with this case.'

'I don't know,' Mrs Honcutt said. 'Of course, if he was a lawyer he could have. My brother, Hervey, insisted on having Mr Stanton come out with him to look after his interests. And I guess Mr Stanton thinks we've got a pretty good case or he wouldn't have gambled on coming – paying all his own expenses and all that. Going to take a percentage if we win.'

'He and your brother are staying at the same hotel with you?' Selby asked.

'That's right. But they're not on the same floor. We wanted to get rooms all together, but we couldn't do it. Hervey's down on the fifth floor, and Mr Stanton is on the same floor with me but he's way down at the other end of the corridor. The manager of the place says that perhaps he can get us closer together a little later on. You see, Hervey and Mr Stanton didn't get in until late last night. On the night train.'

Inez looked at Selby, hesitated a moment, then said, 'Doug, run along, will you? I'm in a horrible mood for social chitchat, and I guess Mrs Honcutt is right. I'll run out and have a cup of hot tea with her. I want to talk to her a little about the case and then I'm going to do a little more work and …'

'And tonight you're going to go to bed,' Mrs Honcutt said. 'It isn't going to do you a mite of good to walk into court tomorrow so tired that your eyes look like two holes burnt in a blanket. You're a mighty attractive young woman, as well as a smart young woman, and there's people on that jury that are going to be looking you over with a lot of approval, and I want you to be looking your best.'

Inez gave Doug a tired smile. 'Wish me luck, Doug.'

Selby hesitated for a moment, then crossed over to grip her hand. 'Luck, Inez,' he said.

CHAPTER ELEVEN

Rex Brandon was still at the courthouse when Selby tapped the ashes out of his pipe on the iron rail which bordered the flight of steps which led to the front door. The other county officials had gone home, but the janitor had not as yet locked the front doors for the night, and Selby climbed the long flight of stairs, looked with nostalgic longing at the double mahogany doors which opened into the courtroom where he had been through so many hard-fought legal battles.

Brandon was relieved to see him, but plainly worried. 'Doug,' he said, 'we've got a bear by the tail and we can't let go.'

Selby glanced at his watch. 'Getting along about dinner-time Rex?'

'I suppose so,' Brandon said, 'but sit down. You've got fifteen or twenty minutes. Light up your pipe and let's talk things over.'

Selby settled comfortably in the chair, elevated his feet to the corner of the sheriff's desk. The sheriff leaned back in his creaking swivel chair, rolled a cigarette, propped his own feet up in the middle of the desk. He grinned across through the friendly haze of tobacco smoke and said, 'Seems like old times, Doug.'

Selby nodded.

For a moment, they smoked in silence, then Selby said, 'You know, Rex, I have an idea that whole thing ties into this will-contest case that's coming up for trial in the Superior Court tomorrow.'

Brandon shook his head and said, 'We've got a bear by the tail, Doug.'

'Just what is it, Rex?'

'Well, we've found some hydrocyanic acid in a little bottle and a medicine dropper.'

'Where?'

'In that waiter's room at the hotel,' Brandon said wearily. 'A little room that he has down in the basement. And I don't like it, Doug.'

'Any fingerprints on the bottle?' Selby asked. 'Any druggist's label, any …'

'That's just the point, Doug. There isn't a single fingerprint on the whole blamed bottle. There's just the bottle and the medicine dropper. There isn't a label on the bottle, nothing to show where he got it or how long he's had it.'

'Looks to me like a plant,' Selby said.

Brandon nodded. 'The way I figure it out is that if that man had wiped his own fingerprints off the bottle so that it couldn't be connected with him, he wouldn't have been foolish enough to have stuck it in the back of his suitcase under some old clothes. He'd have dumped the acid down the sink, washed out the bottle, scrubbed off all the fingerprints, and then thrown the bottle away somewhere. He had plenty of time.'

Selby nodded.

'Well, there you are,' Brandon said.

'Who found the bottle?'

'Otto Larkin and Carl Gifford. They went rummaging around the man's room while I was trying to get something on this Fred Albion Roff. Of course when they found that bottle – well, you know how Larkin is. And Carl Gifford couldn't wait. Soon as they identified the hydrocyanic acid, they rang up the *Blade*. Seen it?'

Selby shook his head.

'It just came out,' Brandon said wearily, 'and you'd think they'd hung up a new world's record solving murder cases. Now, the way I look at it, we've got this Farley, the waiter who took the breakfast up. He has a criminal record, and we've found a bottle of hydrocyanic acid in his room. That's just enough circumstantial evidence to put us in a spot, but the way I see it, Doug, it ain't enough to get a conviction. We haven't any motive and I'm not so sure we can ever prove any motive. What's more, Henry Farley has got old A B Carr as his lawyer, and you know what *that* means.'

'What does Carr say, now that you've discovered the acid.'

Brandon made a gesture of irritation. 'You know Carr. He's shocked. He's deeply pained. It appears to him now that his client is the victim of a conspiracy. He doesn't exactly come right out and say that the *police* are trying to frame his client, but if he can't find some better explanation by the time he comes to trial, that's what it's going to be.'

Selby nodded.

'Any possible connection between this man, Roff, and Farley?'

'That's the thing that bothers me,' the sheriff said. 'Farley was born on the Pacific Coast, and apparently he never left the Pacific Coast. Fred Albion Roff is from the Middle West. He's been out here twice before.'

'What was the reason for his trip this time?' Selby asked.

'Apparently it had something to do with an alimony settlement in Los Angeles. And I guess that's all of it.'

'Then why did he come to Madison City?'

'Now you're asking questions,' Brandon said. 'We may get the answers to some of them within the next hour or two. I have the Los Angeles police working on the thing. Apparently he came here from Los Angeles, and apparently the business that took him West was business that had to do with an alimony settlement. He was representing a husband who had to pay monthly alimony. The woman lives in Los Angeles. From the evidence we have now, it looks as though the woman sort of wants to get married again and is holding off because she didn't want to lose the alimony. The idea was that Roff was going to make her a lump-sum proposition. That's what he was supposed to be working on. Anyway, he was in Los Angeles yesterday.'

'You mean Roff was.'

'That's right. He came here on the early morning bus from Los Angeles. But the woman in the divorce case says he never even came near her. I don't understand it.'

'What have you found out about Roff?'

Brandon said, 'He's a lawyer. He is pretty well fixed, but somehow he doesn't seem to stand too high in the community. He's considered pretty slick. People don't have too much confidence in him. He made a lot of money out of investments. He was shrewd at them. He didn't have a big practice, but all of the cases he did handle were big ones. The man had enough money so he could afford to pick and choose and – well, sort of putting two and two together from the way we get it over the long-distance telephone, Doug, I gather that the rank and file of common people were just a little bit afraid of him. He was just a little *too* smart – sort of a local A B Carr on a penny-ante scale, if you get what I mean.'

Selby laughed and shook his head. 'You still underestimate old A B C, Rex. That man is a genius, a past master of courtroom strategy. He …'

'He's crooked as a dog's hind leg,' Brandon interrupted.

'Probably he is,' Selby said, 'but he's a genius just the same.'

'I don't care how smart a man is, if he ain't honest,' Brandon said with finality, 'that settles it with me.'

Selby said, 'Old A B C isn't exactly dishonest, Rex. He simply has a certain code. He doesn't care what his clients do. He just closes his eyes to that, but the probabilities are that as far as A B C himself is concerned, you'll never catch him doing anything that's actually crooked.'

'You mean we'll never *catch* him,' Brandon said bitterly, 'and you may be right.'

Selby said, abruptly, 'Rex, I wish you'd make a determined effort to trace those two people who got off the train, the two people who were wearing white gardenias. I can't help but think that if we knew the histories of those two people and the reason Carr met them, we might get somewhere.'

'I'm working on it,' Brandon said, 'but I'm not getting much support. Carl Gifford – well, he's got his mind made up. He thinks he has the man who did the job, and it's up to me to get the evidence that will enable him to go into court and get a conviction.'

'Why not put it up to Otto Larkin to get the evidence?' Selby asked, grinning.

Brandon snorted. 'You know Larkin. He's stuck his stomach out and is promenading up and down Main Street telling everybody how *he* didn't let any grass grow under *his* feet. He went right down to make a quick search of that waiter's room. He knew what he was looking for and he found it. As far as Larkin is concerned, he's done his work and he's out taking all of the credit. From now on, he'll rest on his oars. That's the thing that bothers me. If Gifford gets enough evidence to convict him, Larkin and Gifford will be strutting around. But if they don't, they'll throw *me* overboard. I'll be the one that fell down on the job. That's the worst of Gifford. He looks out for number one, and he's an expert at passing the buck.'

'You can't find where this Fred Albion Roff knew anything about the will contest case, or had any connection with Hervey Preston or Martha Otley or ...'

'Not a thing.'

Selby said, 'Anita Eldon apparently stayed overnight in Los Angeles. It occurs to me that perhaps Roff was talking with her last night.'

'Could have been,' Brandon said. 'It's too early yet to go jumping at conclusions. I'm trying to find those two people who got off the train and ...'

Brandon broke off as he heard the rapid tapping of high heels in the corridor. 'Sounds like Sylvia,' he said.

Selby got up and opened the door.

Sylvia Martin's eyes were sparkling with excitement. She didn't waste time in greetings, but her hand squeezed Doug's arm reassuringly. She said, 'I've been working on Fred Albion Roff. You know, I'm local correspondent for one of the Los Angeles newspapers, and they're interested in the thing. If they can make it big enough, they're going to play up that white gardenia angle. You know the way they'll do it, Doug.'

'I suppose so,' Selby said. 'Headlines about THE FLOWER OF DEATH and that sort of stuff.'

'Not quite that bad,' she reassured him. 'That's the way it will get into the Sunday supplement, after six months. But anyway, the point I'm making is that they're interested, and have gone to work, and they've given me something to go on.'

'What?' Brandon asked.

She said, 'Last night, Fred Albion Roff was registered at the Palm Vista Hotel.'

'So *that's* where he stayed,' Brandon said, taking his feet off the desk and reaching for a lead pencil. 'I told the police to sort of check up on it. Did he have any visitors?'

'I don't know,' Sylvia said, 'but I do know one thing.'

'What's that?'

'The record of his telephone bill shows that he rang up Madison City 6982 at eight forty-five and talked for fifteen minutes.'

Brandon whistled.

For a moment Selby didn't get it. 'Madison City 6982,' he repeated, glancing from Sylvia to Rex Brandon.

It was Rex Brandon who refreshed Doug's memory. 'That number,' he said, 'is the number of Inez Stapleton's law office.'

Selby found himself glancing incredulously from Brandon to Sylvia Martin.

Brandon dropped the end of his cigarette into a big brass cuspidor. 'Guess we'll see what *she* has to say,' he said grimly.

'But look here, Rex, Inez wouldn't hold out anything in a murder case. If the man had talked with her ...'

'Don't be too sure,' Brandon said. 'She's a lawyer and she's getting to be a good one. She's mixed up in a will contest case involving a million dollars and if there had been some telephone conversation that she wouldn't want to get out because it would hurt the interest of her client, she's just smart enough and determined enough to keep her mouth shut.'

Sylvia glanced significantly at Rex Brandon.

Brandon reached up and switched out the desk light. 'Want to go, Doug?'

Selby shook his head.

Brandon said to Sylvia Martin, 'I'll let you know, Sylvia.'

'I wish you would. It's my tip and I think I'm entitled to any story that comes out of it. The Los Angeles paper wants me to phone.'

Brandon nodded, 'I'll let you know.'

'You're not going?' Selby asked.

She said somewhat wearily, 'I want to find out what she has to say. My being there would be just like a red flag in front of a bull. We'd *never* find out anything if she thought I was going to get a story out of it.'

'Oh, I don't think she feels quite *that* way,' Brandon said.

'I do,' Sylvia said.

There was a moment of silence. Selby looked at his watch, then he announced, 'You're going to dinner with me, Sylvia.'

Sylvia hesitated for just a moment, then said to Brandon, 'We'll be at that new steak house down on Oak Street, Rex. Will you let me know as soon as you find out?'

Brandon nodded.

'I simply can't believe it,' Doug Selby muttered. 'I was talking with Inez not over half an hour ago.'

Sylvia Martin's silence was significant.

CHAPTER TWELVE

Over a dinner of ground roundsteak, which was all that the bill-of-fare offered in the way of meat, oven-browned potatoes, salad, and two cooked vegetables, Selby studied Sylvia Martin.

'Why the appraisal, Doug?'

Selby said somewhat wistfully, 'I don't like being out of harness, Sylvia. Here you are like a hound on a leash with a hot trail in front of you, and I'm – well, I'm just on the sidelines. I'd like to be in there with you. Makes me realize how much water has run under the bridge.'

'You'll be back, Doug.'

'Probably not as a district attorney,' Selby said.

'No, I suppose not,' she conceded. 'You have got away from the district attorneyship. You'll come back decorated with medals and with a broader background and you'll be in demand as a trial lawyer to handle big litigation. You'll get more and more important, put on weight and dignity, become a big corporation lawyer and smile tolerantly at me when I come in and try and get a story on the new hydroelectric plant merger.'

Selby said, 'You'd get the story, Sylvia.'

'Yes, I suppose I would. You'd let me in past your secretary's secretary, past your secretary, into the inner sanctum. You'd be fat and smug and prosperous and you'd tell me that the new deal that had just been made was the most important thing that had happened in the community in years, bringing cheap electric power to the entire district, assuring the community that big factories would take advantage of the new and improved facilities … Doug, does life have to be like that?'

'Like what, Sylvia?'

'Does success have to make for prosperity, and for fat and smugness?'

'I don't know. Hadn't thought about it that way.'

'Think of it now, Doug. You're going to come back here a hero. You'll succeed in whatever you start out to do. Isn't there something better than merging hydroelectric plants and being a big corporation lawyer? Can't you somehow do things that will make for a better world to live in, a world where people will be freer and happier?'

'But the new hydroelectric plant merger will do all that. There'll be lots of jobs …'

'Jobs!' she interrupted. 'Perhaps that's the trouble. Because of what we went through in the thirties we think too much about jobs and not enough about opportunities.'

Selby said, 'Well, I'm not going to quit my office as a prosperous corporation lawyer and fire my secretary and my secretary's secretary and let that hydroelectric merger go by the board without at least a struggle.'

She smiled at him. 'I guess you'd never quit anything without a struggle. Let's go back to murders and let the hydroelectric merger wait for its proper time in the unfolding history of Madison City and of corporation law.'

They both laughed.

Selby said, 'I wish I could get a line on those two people who got off the train – I just can't get that little old woman out of my thoughts.'

'The one with the white gardenia?'

'Yes. She was such a spry, self-contained little thing. She knew just exactly what she was doing and had her own way of doing it. She'd figured her expenses down to the last penny. She probably gave the Pullman car porter a fifteen-cent tip which she had been clutching in her hand for fifteen minutes before he came around to brush her off. And whether she would have added that extra nickel to the dime probably called for quite a bit of careful deliberation.'

'I know the type,' Sylvia said.

'And yet,' Selby went on, 'she isn't just a type. She's an individual character. She's something all her own — something that's as distinctive and American as a country newspaper, but — well, you just can't imagine her being mixed up in a murder case.'

'You can't for a fact.'

'And she probably isn't,' Selby went on. 'But she certainly must have some incidental connection with it. I'd give a good deal to know just what's back of those white gardenias and Carr's trip to the depot.'

'Well,' she said, 'you'll never find out from A B C.'

Selby said musingly, 'Let's suppose that Roff was intending to meet these two people who were coming on the train. Let's suppose that Roff ordered the white gardenias so that when the train came in he could be on hand to meet the witnesses.'

'Witnesses, Doug?'

'They must have been witnesses,' Selby said, 'I can't place them in any other capacity.'

'Witnesses to what, Doug?'

'I wish I knew.'

'Well, suppose they were witnesses, then what happened?'

'Then A B Carr quietly stepped into the picture and went down and scooped them up into his net.'

Sylvia Martin laid her knife and fork carefully down on her plate. 'Doug, do you realize what you're saying?'

'What?'

'That means that Carr must have known Roff was dead and couldn't have come down to meet the train. He must have known that he was perfectly safe in wearing the white gardenia and appearing as the one to whom the witnesses were supposed to report.'

'Conceding they are witnesses,' Selby said.

'But, Doug, that means that Carr is mixed up in that murder, right up to his eyebrows.'

Selby said cautiously, 'I'm just talking about Roff at the present time, and his reason for ordering the gardenia.'

'Keep talking, Doug.'

'When you put two and two together,' Selby went on, 'Carr's story about what happened to those two passengers from the train is rather elastic so far as the time element is concerned.'

'Trust old A B C for that,' Sylvia said. 'If he gives you an explanation, he'll make it sound logical while he's talking to you, but after you get away from him, you'll find he's left himself a hundred loopholes to crawl through.'

'Let's suppose that he picked the two people up at the train; that he drove directly to the bus depot; that he was there for perhaps five or ten minutes; that he came out and started looking through the restaurants trying to find Anita Eldon. There's still quite a bit of time that isn't accounted for. And I don't think Carr could have learned at the bus depot that the party he wanted had gone to some restaurant unless she'd left some message for him. No one there would have known ...'

'What are you getting at, Doug?'

'I'm wondering,' Selby said, 'if perhaps Carr's search for his client didn't include a visit to the hotel.'

'Well, suppose it had?'

Selby said, 'It's quite possible that while he was there he might have seen Henry Farley.'

'Then you think Farley really did the poisoning?'

'I don't know,' Selby said thoughtfully. 'I'm just trying to reconstruct Carr's moves. I ...'

They heard steps marching down the corridor between booths. Selby raised himself so he could see over the partition and said, 'It's Rex. He looks mad all over.'

Brandon caught Selby's signal, came over to join them.

'Well?' Sylvia Martin asked.

'No comment,' Brandon said.

Her face flushed. 'You mean that you aren't going to tell me ...'

'No,' Brandon said. 'I'm quoting her exact words. "No comment." '

'She wouldn't tell you about the phone call!' Selby exclaimed incredulously.

'That's right.'

'Not a thing about it?'

'Just "No comment." That was all she had to say.'

Selby's face showed the extent of his shocked surprise. 'I simply can't believe it, Rex.'

'Did you tell her about what we'd discovered?' Sylvia asked.

'I told her that I wanted to know about a conversation she had over the telephone with Fred Albion Roff last night. She pretended she didn't know what I was talking about, so then I flashed the record on her, and told her that he'd talked with her office for twenty minutes; that he'd checked out of his hotel and taken an early bus to Madison City, gone to the hotel, registered, and been murdered; that I was investigating the murder and I wanted to know everything I could about a possible motive.'

'And then what?'

'She listened until I'd finished talking, started to say something, then caught herself, thought for a minute, and looked me square in the eyes and said, "No comment." '

'What did you do?' Selby asked. 'Come on in and sit down, Rex, and have something to eat.'

'No, thanks. I'm going home. Dinner's waiting for me there.'

'Well, sit in and have a cup of coffee …'

'No thanks. You've got things to talk about, and my missus is waiting for me. Just thought I'd tell you.'

'I can't believe it,' Selby said.

'I guess I got mad,' the sheriff admitted. 'I told her a thing or two. At first I really couldn't believe my ears, but she got mad and I got mad.'

'Was anyone with her?' Selby asked.

'A woman – nice-looking woman somewhere around sixty-odd. She didn't introduce me.'

'Motherly type with white hair?' Selby asked.

'Yes. Why?'

'Do you suppose the presence of this woman had anything to do with her refusal to give you any information.'

'I don't see how it could have,' the sheriff said, 'and even if it had, it didn't need to cramp her style that bad. She could have told the woman to go out to the other office and wait a minute, or else she could have taken me out there. Before I started talking, I gave her every opportunity to get rid of the client, told her I had something I wanted to ask her about, and that I didn't want to interrupt anything she was doing, but I was in a hurry. But she said to go right ahead, just tell her what it was, so I told her.'

Sylvia said, 'Well, she couldn't have done any worse than that with me. *I'm* going to interview her myself on behalf of the paper.'

'The way I see it,' Brandon said, 'is that she's either covering up something for somebody, in which event she's going to get in bad all round, or she learned something from that telephone conversation she's afraid to have become public.'

'That must be it,' Selby said. 'Poor Inez, I guess she's in something of a pickle.'

'Poor Inez, nothing!' Sylvia stormed. 'She knows Rex Brandon well enough so if it had been anything as confidential as that she could have taken him off to one side and told him what it was all about, and told him she didn't want it to get out, and ...'

Selby shook his head. 'I'm not so sure. She might have done it if only *her* interests had been involved, but she's a lawyer and representing clients.'

'Well,' Brandon said, 'I'm going home. She's made her bed and she can lie in it, as far as I'm concerned. If I find out what that conversation was about I'll spread it all over ...'

'The front pages of the *Clarion*,' Sylvia finished with a smile, as Brandon hesitated.

Brandon included them both in a lopsided grin. 'I'm on my way.'

'Tell your wife I'm going to be up to see her,' Selby said.

'I will. She'll be looking for you. Bring Sylvia along.'

Sylvia laughed. 'I'm a working woman, but if I can make it, I will.'

Brandon's stiff-backed walk as he left the restaurant showed that he was still angry.

'Let's get back to those two witnesses,' Selby said. 'What has been done to locate them, Sylvia?'

'We've covered bus depots and the train, the rooming houses and the hotels, all with no luck.'

'You had a pretty good description?'

'Gosh yes, I could almost draw a picture of them. I certainly looked them over because I wanted to pick up a human interest story if I could.'

Selby said, 'Let's do a little detective work, Sylvia.'

Her eyes twinkled. 'I was hoping you'd get around to that.'

Selby grinned. 'Let's start out with a tentative assumption. Let's assume that Carr's meeting of those people at the train was not accidental. Let's assume that Roff had originally intended to meet them. Now, let's suppose that Roff's presence here had something to do with that will contest case.'

'You keep coming back to that case, Doug.'

'That conversation with Inez Stapleton would seem to clinch it, to my mind,' Selby said.

'I suppose so. Of course she *could* be representing a client with an interest in something else – perhaps that alimony settlement.'

'All I'm getting so far is a working hypothesis,' Selby said. 'It may be wrong. It may turn out to be right, but let's first get certain assumptions that seem to be logical and then state them in an orderly sequence.'

'All right. You've made an assumption. It sounds logical. So what comes next?'

'It seems to me that it's fair to assume that these two people who got off the train and were met by Carr were witnesses to something. In that case, they're either witnesses favourable to Carr, or witnesses that are unfavourable.' Sylvia nodded.

'The most logical explanation is that they are unfavourable. If they were favourable, Carr wouldn't have seen they were spirited out of the country. But so far we can't afford to reach any definite decision on that. We have to consider both possibilities.

'Now, let's first assume that they were unfavourable witnesses. Then Carr would want to get them out of the country where they couldn't be reached until after the will contest case had been decided.

'On the other hand, let's suppose they were favourable. Then Carr's logical move would have been to sew up their testimony in the form of an affidavit, and then only take reasonable

94

precautions to see they weren't tampered with until he was ready to put them on the stand.'

Selby waited for Sylvia's comment.

'But if they were unfavourable witnesses, Doug, would they have let Carr rush them out of the country?'

'That depends upon whether they appreciated the significance of their testimony.'

'But do you think that Carr could have taken advantage of a murder ...'

'Don't get me wrong on that, Sylvia. All that I am considering is the possibility that Fred Albion Roff was working with old A B Carr, that he was to have met a certain train; that perhaps Carr didn't entirely trust Roff and was keeping an eye on him. Now let's suppose that Roff was murdered by some person or persons whose identity is unknown. Let's suppose, just for the sake of the argument, that this waiter, Henry Farley, went back to get the tray of breakfast things and found Roff lying dead on the floor. For obvious reasons, and in view of the man's record, he didn't want to be the one to discover the body. And that's supposing he had nothing to do with the murder. Now, under those circumstances, what would he have done?'

'You mean he hurriedly left the room, rushed to a telephone, got hold of Carr and told him that he simply had to see him?'

'Something like that. He may or may not have known that Carr and Roff had any connection.'

Sylvia Martin was nodding thoughtful acquiescence.

'So Farley told Carr that Roff was dead. Carr told Farley to keep quiet; that if he were picked up by the police, he was to say nothing, but telephone for Carr; that Carr would then appear, go through the motions of rebuking the man for not having told his story to the police, and make profuse apologies.'

'What would be the idea of all that, Doug?'

'The idea would be that Farley never would have told *his* story. The police would never have had any statement from him. Carr would go to Brandon, be very apologetic, tell Brandon what Farley's story would have been if Farley had talked, and then immediately asked for a writ of *habeas corpus*, and tell Farley that there was no need for him to do any more talking because Carr had already talked to him.'

Sylvia nodded her head. 'You've convinced me, Doug. What do we do next?'

'In one case,' Selby said, 'the witnesses are being held in some outlying hotel. In the other case, they've probably been driven to some nearby city and put on a bus for some remote destination. How much gasoline have you got, Sylvia?'

'Enough,' she said, pushing back her plate. 'When do we start?'

'Now.'

CHAPTER THIRTEEN

The Palace Hotel at Flora Vista was a three-storey frame building surrounded by huge shade trees. Its long, wide verandas, cupolas and ornamental balconies bore silent witness to a bygone school of architecture.

It was nearly eleven o'clock when Selby and Sylvia Martin entered the high-ceilinged lobby. The lights had already been dimmed, and only an area back of the desk was brightly lighted.

The monotonous repetition of a question which had hitherto been futile gave Selby's voice a flat, expressionless quality as he asked his routine question. 'Sometime today did a woman check in here, dressed in black, around sixty to sixty-five years of age, hair grey but not entirely white, dark, deep-set eyes, and perhaps wearing a white gardenia corsage? This is Miss Martin of the Madison City *Clarion* and we're trying to locate ...'

'Guess you mean Hattie Irwin, don't you?'

'Registered from some place in Kansas?' Selby asked with a sudden surge of expression in his voice.

'Empalma, Kansas, that's right.'

Selby struggled to keep excitement from his voice. 'We'd like to talk with her. Is she in her room?'

'In her room and probably gone to bed,' the clerk said. 'She was down in the lobby about an hour ago and said it was about her bedtime.'

'Give her a ring,' Selby said, and then added, 'It's important.'

The man hesitated a moment, then plugged in a line, very briefly pressed the key, and waited.

Within a second or two he said, 'Mrs Irwin, there are two people in the lobby who would like to see you … Yes … A woman and a man … They say it's important … Very well, I'll tell them.'

He pulled out the plug and said, 'She said to wait five minutes and then to come up. Three-o-two.'

Selby nodded his thanks. He could feel Sylvia Martin's fingers pressing his arm just above the elbow.

'Happen to have a man here, also from Kansas?' he asked. 'Someone who registered today. About …'

'No one else from Kansas registered today. We only had two men. One of them is a travelling salesman from San Francisco; the other one is a man from Denver. I'm quite well acquainted with the travelling salesman. The Denver man is strange.'

'Somewhere past fifty, rather stooped …'

'No, he's about thirty-five, dark hair, grey eyes …'

'Guess he isn't our man,' Selby said. 'We can probably find out what we want from Mrs Irwin.'

Selby strolled away from the desk and guided Sylvia Martin to a leather-lined chair in the dim recesses of the huge lobby, where they would be out of the earshot of the clerk.

Sylvia perched herself on the rounded arm of the chair. 'Gosh, Doug, I'm too excited to sit down and relax. Won't it be a swell break if we can get something that will tie Carr in with that murder and …'

'Take it easy,' Selby cautioned. 'All we know right now is that we've acted on a hypothesis and have achieved a first objective by a process of dead reckoning. But we don't know what lies back of that first objective. We're going to have to use our eyes, our ears, and our heads.'

'Well, at least we're going to find out what Carr had to say to her. That's going to be worth something. We've quit speculating on cold clues and have hit a really hot trail.'

'And where it's going to lead is anyone's guess,' Selby said. 'Come on, let's go up. By the time we get there it will at least have approached the five minutes we were supposed to wait.'

They entered the automatic elevator and rattled and swayed up to the third floor. Selby knocked on the door of room 302.

Hattie Irwin had evidently been in bed when the telephone rang, but she had gone about her preparations to receive visitors with all the proprieties carefully observed. She had utilized the short interval to make the bed, smooth down the counterpane. She had put on a dress, although her feet were encased in bedroom slippers, and her grey hair was smoothed primly back from her forehead. Her deep-set black eyes regarded her two visitors appraisingly and then lighted as they regarded Doug Selby.

'Well, I'll declare!' she exclaimed.

Selby smiled. 'I was on the train with you, Mrs Irwin.'

'I remember you. I noticed you two or three times – a nice-looking figure in your uniform. I have a grandson in the service. Just a private, but he's a nice boy, a mighty nice boy. I haven't seen him in his uniform, but I'll bet he looks really handsome. You're a – a captain?'

'A major,' Selby said. 'And this is Miss Sylvia Martin. She's a newspaper reporter.'

'Well, well, a newspaper reporter, eh? Won't you sit down. How did you happen to find *me* here, and what do you want?'

'Just a little information,' Selby said. 'You see, Miss Martin is on the newspaper at Madison City, and you got off the train at Madison City.'

'That's right. That was this morning about ten-forty, I believe it was. We were supposed to be in there at ten thirty-two, but we were eight and a half minutes late.'

'That's right,' Selby said, smiling at Sylvia Martin. 'You have friends in Madison City, Mrs Irwin?'

'Land sakes, how would I have any friends in Madison City? This is the first time in my life I was ever out of Kansas except once when I went to Iowa.'

'But someone met you at the train?' Selby prompted.

'Oh yes. That was a man from the touring agency. Well, guess he wasn't either. I guess there was some mistake made, when you come right down to it.'

'Did you get his name?' Selby asked.

She said, 'No I didn't. You see, there was some sort of a mix up.'

Sylvia Martin's voice was kindly. 'Could you tell me what it was, Mrs Irwin.'

'Well,' the woman said, 'you see when I won this trip to California …'

'*Won* a trip to California?' Sylvia interrupted.

She nodded her head, her manner showing intense satisfaction. 'Just like rolling off a log.'

'Suppose you tell us first what happened when you arrived in Madison City,' Selby said. 'I believe you pinned on a white gardenia corsage just before you got off the train, didn't you?'

'That's right.'

'And that was to enable you to meet someone? It was to identify you in some way?'

'That's right. A man from the tour was to meet me there. Seems like there were two of us on the train, but I didn't know the other man was there. He'd been travelling up in the day coach. Land sakes, I don't know how a body could travel that way – but that was the sort of trip he'd won and I guess he liked it better than staying at home. He didn't make as high a rating as I did, I guess. They tell me I was mighty near perfect – right around ninety-eight per cent, I think the man said.'

Selby exchanged glances with Sylvia Martin. 'Perhaps you'd better tell us about this contest, Mrs Irwin.'

'There wasn't anything to it. It was one of those things that come in the mail. It didn't cost anything to try, there was a stamped addressed envelope already enclosed, and all you had to do was to answer some questions and see how many faces you could find concealed in a drawing. You know, a picture of some trees and a farm and a wagon, and you'd turn it upside down and you'd find a woman's face in part of the wagon, or a man's face in the trees.'

Her index finger moved in little tracing motions as she enthusiastically recounted her triumph, drawing imaginary pictures in the air.

'And then what happened?' Selby asked.

'Well, I answered the questions and picked out the faces and sent it in. I didn't know whether I'd done so good, but the next thing I knew, the man from the company called me up and he seemed all excited. He asked me to come to meet him at the hotel and told me I'd won a first prize – a trip to California with all expenses paid. But I had to leave almost right away because of trouble with Pullman reservations. You know, I've been sort of worrying about that.'

'About what?'

'Well, with the way travel is now there isn't supposed to be any non-essential travel and this company seemed a little worried about that. They'd fixed up the contest some time ago, before travel got so tight and one of their prizes was a trip to California, and – well they were a little worried about it. About how people would feel about it in case it came out.'

'So they asked you not to say anything about it?' Sylvia asked sympathetically.

'Well, not to talk about it. And he just said to get my things packed and – they said there wasn't anything to conceal, but I just didn't need to go around telling everybody right where I was going.'

'I see,' Selby said, 'and they gave you a ticket?'

'That's right, first-class ticket, Pullman ticket, and gave me money to eat on the dining car. Even figured out everything including a tip to the porter. But, lands sakes, they must have thought I was a millionaire the way they wanted me to go around tipping porters. I didn't give that porter as much as they thought I should, I guess, but the railroad company is paying him a salary for doing his work, and that's all he did, just his work.'

'Now, the name of this company?' Selby asked.

'Land sakes, I don't even know. It was some kind of a breakfast food company that wanted to advertise a new type of breakfast food. Something I've never heard of before and I don't see what good they expected to get out of sending me to California. Of course, they said that where they have thousands of people taking part in a contest, they get a certain amount of advertising out of it, but me, I swear I didn't even remember the name of the food they were advertising.'

'And the representative of the company – did he accompany you?'

'Oh no. He told me that I was to be turned over to some touring agency. Seems that's the way those big companies do. They can't afford to handle the tours themselves, but there are touring agencies that make a speciality of those things, so the advertising agencies just turn their people over to the touring agencies.'

'And when you got to Madison City you were to wear a white gardenia so as to identify yourself?'

'That's right.'

'And the man from the touring agency would also wear a white gardenia, I suppose.'

'That's what they said.'

'And when you got to Madison City this man from the touring agency picked you up and took you in charge?'

'That's right.'

'And brought you over here?'

'That's it. This is where we stay the first night. Now, I don't know just how long we're going to stay here. The man from the touring agency seemed a little bit indefinite about it, but after all, it isn't costing me a cent, and I'm getting a regular tour out of it. I have a niece in Sacramento and I asked the man if we were going up there. He said he didn't know for sure, it depended on the way things were now. Travel conditions are terribly upset, you know, but he's been very nice to me.'

'He left you here?'

'Got me a room here, yes.'

Selby frowned. 'He couldn't have driven you over here right after you left the train, Mrs Irwin. There wasn't time enough for him to have done that and –'

'Oh, that man that met me at the train wasn't the one. That was a mistake.'

Selby saw Sylvia Martin's face lose some of its animation as the full import of Mrs Irwin's remark hit her.

'You say he wasn't the one?' Selby asked.

'Heavens sakes, no. That was just a mistake. The way it turned out, he was looking for somebody else, but he saw me with my white gardenia and he came over and talked to me, and said I was to go with him. And then he saw this other man that had won the second prize in the contest, and so he picked us both up to take us uptown. He seemed to be very nice.'

'And then what happened?' Selby asked.

She said, 'It turned out that there'd been a mix-up. The man that was to have met us was delayed a little bit. He found us sitting there in the automobile. The man that picked us up had gone to the bus depot and ...'

Selby interrupted, his voice quickened with interest. 'As I gather it, it turned out that this man who picked you up at the station was looking for someone else? Is that right?'

'That's right.'

'How long was he in the bus depot?'

'Oh, quite a little while I guess. I don't know. We'd been sitting there in the car about ten minutes before this man that was to have met us showed up then and he was very apologetic.'

'Was he wearing a white gardenia?'

'No he wasn't. He knew us all right though, because he had found out we'd left the depot in this man's automobile. He drove up alongside and he was very sorry about everything, and he said we were to get in with him; that he was from the touring company and that he'd been a little bit late.'

'So you transferred from one automobile to the other?'

'That's right.'

'Both of you?'

'Yes.'

'And then what?'

'And then we came right over here and he put us in the hotel.'

'The man that won the second prize?' Selby asked. 'Do you know who he was?'

'Yes, his name was – now wait a minute. It's a funny name. Something like Castle. I always think of Castle when I think of it – Hastle – that's it, H-a-s-t-l-e, Carl Hastle.'

'And what became of him? He didn't stay at this hotel?'

'No, he'd won a different kind of trip from what I had. Not so good. He had a second prize. I'd won the first prize. I just can't realize that out of all the people who sent in the answers that I –'

'And I take it,' Selby said, 'that the man who represented the tours left you here, and then went on with this man Hastle?'

She looked at him blankly and shook her head.

'You don't know where Hastle went?'

'No. The man from the touring agency took care of that.'

Selby flashed Sylvia Martin a warning glance. 'Then the man from the touring agency is staying on here at the hotel?'

'That's right.'

'Man about thirty-five with dark hair and grey eyes?' Selby asked casually.

'Yes. His name is Mr Floris. He seems to be a very nice man.'

'You don't know what room he's in?'

'Well, now I just don't. I know he took me here to the hotel and told me I was to register, and then he went to get some gasoline for his automobile, and when he got back I'd already been taken up to this room. He had some other matters to attend to. I didn't see him only once or twice during the day. He says that on a tour of this sort you have to get things kind of organized and he has to find out from his home company ...'

'Just a minute,' Selby said. 'You wait right there. You want to stay with her, Sylvia?'

'I do not,' Sylvia Martin said. 'I want to go with you. You wait right here, Mrs Irwin, we'll be back. There's one very important thing we have to find out about.'

Selby and Sylvia Martin left the perplexed woman rather abruptly. They dashed for the elevator, went down to the lobby.

The clerk looked up from a magazine.

'Say,' Selby said, as though an idea had just occurred to him, 'that man from Denver that registered wasn't Floris, was he?'

'That's right, Elmer D Floris.'

'Well, can you beat that?' Selby exclaimed. 'What room's he in?'

'Three-o-four.'

'Don't ring him,' Selby said. 'Isn't this a coincidence? It shows what a small world it is after all.'

Back in the elevator it seemed that the slow-moving cage never would get to the third floor.

'Right in the adjoining room,' Sylvia Martin whispered. 'Doug, do you suppose he could hear us?'

'You can't tell,' Selby said. 'He must have heard the telephone ring. Hang it, if he's slipped through our fingers …'

'But that means Carr was telling the truth, doesn't it?' Sylvia Martin asked.

Selby grinned. 'It means that if he has to he can verify every fact he told us. This man Floris is the one who will break the chain leading to Carr …'

'Doug, if that's the case, why didn't Carr have Floris – ?'

The elevator lurched to a stop with interminable slowness, the automatic mechanism released the door and slid it back in a series of jerks.

Selby and Sylvia almost ran down the corridor.

'Stand to one side of the centre of the door,' Selby said. 'We don't know just what we're getting into.'

He knocked on the door of 304.

There was no answer.

Selby knocked again.

There was no sound of motion from the inside of the room.

Selby tried the knob of the door.

The knob turned freely. The door was unlocked. It swung open and after a moment Selby moved his arm around the door jamb to grope for the light switch on the wall. He found it and switched on the light.

The room was empty, but there was the smell of fresh cigar smoke and an open magazine lay face down on the table.

Selby entered the room. His hand pressed down on the cushion of the chair beside the table.

'Still warm,' he said.

'What does that mean?' Sylvia asked. 'Do you think he …'

'Our bird has flown,' Selby said. 'He could either hear our conversation in the adjoining room through the wall, or he had some sort of a listening device that he put up against the wall of the closet.'

Selby moved over to the telephone, snatched up the receiver, waited for several seconds before the night clerk's leisurely hello came over the wire.

Selby's voice was sharp with authority. 'If this man who registered under the name of Elmer Floris comes down to the desk,' he said, 'detain him until I get there, I'm coming right down.'

He didn't give the surprised clerk any opportunity to reply, but slammed up the receiver and once more made a dash for the elevator. This time they found the elevator was back down at the ground floor and rather than wait for it, Selby found the stairs, went dashing down them two at a time, his pell-mell descent sounding like a rushing avalanche on the wooden staircase.

The face of the clerk showed bewilderment and suspicion. 'Say,' he demanded, 'what's all this about? I thought you said you knew the man.'

'Has he checked out?'

'He must have been waiting to take the elevator down the minute you got up there.'

'And you let him pay his bill and …'

'The bill was all paid. He paid in advance. What's the idea, anyway?'

Selby grabbed the desk telephone. 'Connect us with long distance,' he said, 'and get me the sheriff at Madison City just as fast as you can put the call through. Tell them it's a major emergency and we want action.'

It was less than a minute before Selby heard Rex Brandon's drawling voice over the telephone.

'Rex,' Selby said, 'we're at Flora Vista at the Palace Hotel. A man you want has just checked out of here. He's around thirty-five years old, dark hair, slate-grey eyes, dressed in … just a minute. Hold the line.'

Selby turned from the mouthpiece to the clerk. 'How was he dressed?'

'Sort of a pin-striped, blue business suit.'

'Overcoat?'

'Had one over his arm.'

'A bag?'

'That's right, light travelling bag.'

Selby relayed the description over the telephone. 'He'll probably be travelling by private automobile. Put out a dragnet, Rex. We'll tell you more when we get back to Madison City. Start the police working on it and get the highway patrol on the job. The man's going under the name of Elmer D Floris, but that's probably an alias.'

Brandon's voice was crisp with authority. 'Okay, Doug, I'll get busy on the wire right away. When will you tell me what it's all about?'

'As soon as we can get back there,' Selby said. 'We'll have a passenger with us. Better wait at the office.'

Selby hung up the telephone, said to the clerk, 'We're going back up to Mrs Irwin's room. If she tries to check out – you'd better go up, Sylvia, I'll wait here in the lobby.'

'What do I tell her?' Sylvia Martin asked.

'She's going back to Madison City with us,' Selby said, 'and don't tell her too much. As far as she's concerned, it's just a part of her tour.'

CHAPTER FOURTEEN

The little group sat around the desk in Rex Brandon's office. Hattie M Irwin was frankly puzzled but nevertheless made no attempt to disguise the fact that she was more pleased than otherwise to find herself the centre of so much attention.

'Now, as I understand it,' Brandon said, when she had finished, 'you simply filled out the blank in this contest and sent it in.'

'That's right.'

'And then this man telephoned you and told you he was a representative of the company and that you had won a prize.'

'The *first* prize,' she announced proudly. 'He was the president of the company.'

'And that the first prize consisted of a trip to California with all expenses paid.'

'That's right.'

Brandon looked across at Selby, 'You want to question her about it, Doug?'

Selby said, 'You do it, Rex.'

Brandon hesitated for a moment. 'I think you could do better than I could, Doug.'

'Your questions are official. Mine aren't.'

'We can make them official.'

Selby merely smiled.

Brandon took a deep breath, 'Now, you came from Empalma?'

'That's right.'

'Did you know a man by the name of Roff, Fred Albion Roff?'

'I didn't know him, but I've heard of the name. I've seen it in the newspaper. He's a big lawyer there.'

'You don't remember ever having seen him?'

'No.'

'Ever been a witness in a lawsuit?'

'No.'

Brandon pulled a sheet of paper toward him on which several names had been written. 'Do you know a woman lawyer named Inez Stapleton, here?'

'No.'

'Do you know anyone in California?'

'I have a niece in Sacramento. She's the only one I know here.'

'Did you know a Martha Otley?'

'No.'

'An Eleanor Preston?'

'No.'

'A Barbara Honcutt?'

'No.'

'Hervey Preston?'

'No.'

'Now, this man Hastle who was on the train with you. What do you know about him?'

'Nothing. I hadn't met him until we got off the train at Madison City. And then this man that had the white gardenia spoke to me and ...'

'What did he say?'

'He smiled very courteously and said, "Are you the person I'm looking for?"'

'And what did you say?'

'Well, naturally I told him I was, because he was the representative of the travel bureau.'

110

'And what did he say?'

'He said that he had a car waiting there, and if I'd just come with him he'd take me uptown and then he saw this other man with the white gardenia, and he said, "That's strange" and walked over to the man and said, "Are you looking for me?" And the man said he was and the gentleman seemed sort of puzzled for a minute and then said, "Well, come on and we'll get in the car."'

'Did he ask you your name?'

'Going uptown he asked me if I was … Now I can't be sure of the name.'

'Anita Eldon?' Selby supplemented.

'It sounds something like that.'

'And what did you tell him?'

'I told him I was Mrs Irwin. And then he thought for a minute and then asked the man what his name was, and that was when the man said his name was Carl Hastle. That was the first time I'd heard it. And then one thing led to another and it turned out that there'd been some sort of a mistake made and I suggested perhaps he'd better take us back to the depot, but he said he thought it would be better for us to go to the hotel and wait there.'

'What did Hastle say?'

'Not much of anything.'

Brandon glanced speculatively across at Doug Selby.

'You're sure you don't know Martha Otley or Eleanor Preston?'

'Never heard of them before.'

'Do you know anyone in McKeesville, Kansas?'

'I've never been there.'

'Don't know anyone in Madison City?'

'No.'

'This man, Elmer Floris, who picked you up. Did he tell you anything about himself?'

'Not much. He was a very glib talker though. He kept talking almost all the time about the scenery and about the beauties of California, and asking me questions about Kansas.'

'What part of Kansas?'

'Oh, just general questions.'

'Ask you about any people?'

'No.'

'And you're certain you don't know anything about Fred Albion Roff?'

'You mean the lawyer from Empalma?'

'Yes.'

'Only I've just read about him in the paper.'

'Do you remember what you've read?'

'No. Just things he'd say. He'd make speeches at banquets and things like that.'

'Do you remember anything he said in his speeches?'

'Lord no. They were just speeches – you know, the sort of things people say when they're standing up after dinner.'

'You're a widow?'

'That's right.'

'Any children?'

'Not living. My son died. I have a grandson in the Army.'

'How long have you been a widow?'

'Thirteen years.'

'Do you have any property of your own?'

The lips clamped together. 'That's none of your business,' she snapped.

Selby grinned. 'What I mean is have you supported yourself by working or ...'

'I've supported myself, and before my husband died I supported him. He was sick for a long while, and if I do say it myself as I shouldn't, he didn't want for a thing.'

'Where have you worked?'

'Various places.'

'What sort of work?'

'Mostly general housework.'

'Where were you employed at the time you sent in your answer to this contest?'

'I don't see what all that has to do with it.'

Selby's smile was most gracious. 'Neither do I,' he admitted. 'I'm just trying to get a background, because it may be that it may have some bearing on the matter we're investigating.'

'Well,' she said, 'I don't know just what it's all about, but as far as I'm concerned I was getting along very nicely. I'd won a trip to California and I'd had all my expenses paid. This Mr Floris was very nice and he was going to take me to Sacramento where I'd see my niece. Now what are *you* going to do about it?'

Selby glanced quizzically at Brandon.

The sheriff elevated his elbow and started scratching the hair along the back of his neck.

'What *are* you going to do about it?' Mrs Irwin demanded.

'Ma'am,' the sheriff blurted, 'I'll be darned if I know.'

'Well, I'm certainly not going to spend *my* hard-earned money. I had a trip to California and back all paid for, and here I am. You folks have interfered with that trip and I'm looking to you to see that you make up to me what I've lost. If you've frightened Mr Floris away, why that's up to you. That was the last thing Mrs Kensett said to me. She was the woman I was working for when I got the prize. She said, "I don't mind your quitting, Hattie, not under any circumstances, but you must be certain that those people don't get you out to California and then leave you high and dry. Now you must hold them to it." And that's what I'm doing, Sheriff. I don't want to be difficult, but I'm going to have my trip to California and back. I've won it and I want it.'

Brandon shifted his position uncomfortably. 'Well now, Ma'am,' he said, 'I don't know just what we can do. I've got to talk with the district attorney, but I have an idea we can hold you as a material witness, and doing that, we naturally pay your expenses while we're holding you. And I guess it's all right for us to put you up at a hotel, at least for the time being. Anyway, that's what I'm going to do. What do you think, Doug?'

Selby said, 'I hate to let you down, Rex, but my thoughts aren't the thoughts of Madison County right now, and if I expressed my thoughts the chances are that Carl Gifford would have thoughts of his own that were one hundred per cent different.'

'That's right,' the sheriff admitted. 'Okay, Ma'am, I'm going to put you in a hotel. But remember, that you aren't to go away. You're being held as a material witness.'

'Witness to what?' she snapped.

'Now,' Brandon admitted, 'you've got me. I'm darned if I know.'

CHAPTER FIFTEEN

Selby spent the morning with Rex Brandon. The sheriff with painstaking patience, sat at the telephone, trying to pick up loose threads by tireless attention to detail. No automobile of the type driven by Elmer D Floris had been registered in the state to any party of that name. A thorough search of Flora Vista disclosed that no one by the name of Floris had registered at any of the rooming houses or hotels after Floris had abruptly left the Palace Hotel, nor had any outgoing bus carried a passenger who answered Floris' description. The police reported they had made prompt inquiries following Brandon's telephone call. It was, of course, quite possible that those inquiries had been made in the half-hearted manner of someone performing a routine task.

Brandon had, however, put in the morning supplementing those police inquiries with a more careful check-up. His results had been absolutely nil.

Carl Gifford had been in shortly before noon. His manner radiated assurance. Henry Farley had been charged with first degree murder and A B Carr was going to represent him. Because Carr was tied up in court in a will contest case, it was stipulated that a preliminary hearing could be had the following afternoon after court had adjourned. Carr had given Gifford his unofficial assurance that he would make no attempt to get Farley released on the preliminary examination. The evidence, the old criminal lawyer had reluctantly conceded, was sufficient to cause any unbiased magistrate to bind Farley over for trial. And, that being the case, Carr would consent to make the preliminary hearing a mere matter of form, although Carr continued to protest the innocence of his client.

Brandon had displayed some uneasiness. 'I'm sort of figuring where that leaves us,' he had explained when Gifford had questioned his lack of enthusiasm.

'Leaves us right on top of the heap,' Gifford had said. 'We have such an open-and-shut case against the man that Carr can't put on any fight.'

'On the other hand,' Brandon suggested, 'it puts us in the position of having one particular bear by the tail. If we ever have to let go, we're going to have a hard time finding a place to light.'

'We aren't going to have to let go.'

'Well, you can't ever tell. Seems to me we're jumping at a lot of conclusions here. The fact that old A B Carr walks into court tomorrow afternoon and just goes through the motions, then lets the Judge bind Farley over, means that we're definitely committed to try Farley for the murder.'

'Well, why not?'

'Because we haven't got enough evidence to convict him.'

'We will have by the time we go to trial,' Gifford declared confidently. 'We'll pick up more evidence here and there. We'll show motive and opportunity. We'll show the means of death and then bring the poison home to Farley. I don't know what more you'll want than that.'

'Suppose we don't pick up any additional evidence?' the sheriff had insisted doggedly.

'We will.'

'I'm not so certain. Looks to me as though Carr is kind of rushing us into something here. We get suspicious of Farley. We ask him a few questions and he acts as though we were trying to give him a third degree and telephones for Carr. Carr comes in with an explanation that really doesn't explain, and then goes and gets a writ of *habeas corpus*. Then we uncover some other evidence which, when you come right down to it, is the *only* real evidence we've got, and we file a murder charge and Carr says carelessly, "Oh, yes, I'm trying another case. We'll just go through the motions of a preliminary hearing and bind this man over." Sort of looks to me as though Carr had set in the background but forced us to pick on this man Farley for the murder. And it just may be that that's exactly what Carr wants. Once we've picked Farley as our choice we're going to have a heck of a time backing up and trying to pin the thing on somebody else.'

Gifford flushed, swung around to face Selby, started to say something, then changed his mind.

Brandon had interpreted the expression of Gifford's face. 'Of course, I don't know any law, I just know a little bit about how foxy old A B Carr is. I'm giving you just my opinion.'

'Yours and who else's?' Gifford asked sarcastically.

Brandon got to his feet. 'Nobody's.'

Gifford turned on his heel, paused at the door of the office to fling over his shoulder, 'Suppose you come down to earth, and start working on Roff and Farley. Check their backgrounds and you'll find they have some connection. Put your effort in on digging out a motive and you'll find one. *You* get the evidence, and *I'll* present it and secure a conviction.'

Gifford went out slamming the door angrily behind him.

Selby, feeling like a man who had been put out of his own house, waited for another ten or fifteen minutes, smoking silently, listening to the sheriff's telephone conversations. Then, making his departure elaborately casual, Selby said, 'Well, guess I'll get a bite of lunch and look in on the trial of that will contest case and see how it's coming along.'

Selby's manner hadn't deceived the old sheriff. 'I got more confidence in you, son, than all the rest of these other fellows put together,' Brandon blurted. 'I'm running this office. Don't you let anybody say anything that hurts your feelings or causes you to get out. You stick right around here. We'll work on this case together. That is, as much time as you've got to spare.'

Selby smiled. 'Thanks, Rex, but I have a few things to attend to and there's not much good I can do here. I was up most of the night and I think I'll celebrate my freedom from responsibility by a siesta.'

Selby resolutely refrained from calling Sylvia Martin when he awakened about three in the afternoon. He strolled into court about half past three.

Judge Fairbanks was presiding over the trial with an air of grave impartiality. A jury had already been selected and evidence was being put on. Old A B Carr had apparently finished with his preliminary proofs and was standing, tall and graceful, his finely chiselled face and wavy grey hair giving him the dignified appearance of a courtroom aristocrat.

W Barclay Stanton was standing in the middle of the courtroom floor, his deep voice booming out fatiguing platitudes, while the jurors regarded him with a certain detached curiosity. Inez Stapleton sat at the counsel table, her fingers impatiently twisting and twirling at a pencil. Mrs Honcutt was seated at the right of Inez, her face turned from the jury.

Over behind old A B Carr, sat a young woman whom, at first, Selby failed to recognize. Only as he made a second appraisal did he realize that this demure, plainly dressed young woman who sat with downcast eyes, her hair combed severely back from her forehead, was the glamorous Anita Eldon whom Selby and Sylvia Martin had studied in the restaurant the day before.

Court took a ten-minute adjournment while Selby was sizing up the situation, and amid the hubbub of low-pitched voices and the shuffling steps of spectators filing out of the courtroom, Selby heard Inez Stapleton's voice calling his name.

He crossed over to the corner of the courtroom where she was standing in a little space that at the moment was clear of spectators.

'Oh, Doug,' she said, laughing nervously, 'it's absolutely ghastly.'

'What is?'

'Do you see what he's done with that woman? He's worked over her as a master director would work over a skilful actress and he's certainly drilled her in the part she's to play. She's the most demure, sweetest little thing, and her clothes look so simple! But don't worry that she hasn't got on nylon stockings and she's learned a trick of always holding her toe down when she has her knees crossed so that it gives the jurors just the right perspective on her legs. Not too much you know. She's too demure and modest to know anything about cheesecake! So sweet, and so incapable of coping with the big, bad world, now that Mother is dead. And you should see old Alfonse B Carr when he walks over to confer with her. He bends down as deferentially as though he were looking at some fragile flower of rare beauty, and she raises her eyes so trustingly at him and smiles so warmly, and shakes her head. A perfect pantomime of a lawyer asking his client a question, his fatherly solicitude indicating his belief that she embodies all that is just and good and right in the world, and she looks up at him with that trusting expression and then shakes her head, as though to tell him she can't cope with all this sordid commercialism of these dreadful people on the other side, and he'll just have to use his judgement. And Carr reassuringly pats her hand and – it's a perfect pantomime of saying, "Don't worry, dear, this jury won't let the big, bad man steal your money." Damn him, I suppose he's been rehearsing her in that the whole morning.'

'And probably a good part of the night, to boot,' Selby said. 'Don't ever underestimate Carr or his courtroom technique. While you were digging away in law books trying to find some legal doctrine that would be of some help, old A B Carr was picking out clothes for his client, and probably rehearsing that touching little scene a couple of hundred times. He'll think of a new one tonight and there'll be a fresh tableau for the jurors in the morning. How's W Barclay Stanton doing?'

'He's doing plenty,' she said. 'You can't head the old walrus off. He's belching words all over the courtroom. Standing up with what he thinks is his chest pushed way out in front and proclaiming unctuous platitudes in the oratorical voice of a rural spellbinder. Just watch the jurors. They look at him for a while as though they were looking at some new sort of animal in a cage and then just when Stanton is making some point, Carr will walk over to his client and bend over her with that air of tender solicitude, and every eye in the courtroom will follow him. Stanton can't hold their attention when that happens. It's a perfect spiritual striptease. Damn the man, I hate him.'

'Hating him isn't going to do your client any good,' Selby said. 'You're going to have to sell your client to that jury. You've got her in the wrong place. She's sitting so she faces you and her back is half turned to the jury. Put her around where W Barclay Stanton is sitting and let the jury look at her placid countenance. Let them see *her* smile once in a while. Let her put her hand on your arm in a motherly way, and ...'

'Bunk!' Inez interrupted. 'Do you think W Barclay Stanton would move from that chair? I tried to explain to him that it would be better to have my client sitting over on that side of us. He says that he wants to be where the jury can watch *his* face.

120

His face my foot! I could brain the man if I had a club and there was anything in his head to work on.'

Selby laughed, then instantly became serious. 'Understand you wouldn't answer a question the sheriff asked you last night, Inez.'

Instantly her face became wooden. 'I couldn't give him the answer he wanted to the question he asked.'

'You had a telephone conversation with Fred Albion Roff?'

'Are you asking for yourself, Doug, for Rex, or – or for the *Madison City Clarion*?'

Selby said thoughtfully, 'I'm asking for you, Inez.'

'Just what do you mean?'

'I want to give you a chance to get into the clear.'

'And if you knew the answer, I suppose you'd tell your friend, Rex Brandon?'

'Perhaps.'

'And Sylvia Martin?'

'I don't know.'

'If you didn't, Rex would.'

'Perhaps.'

'No comment,' Inez said truculently.

'You know,' Selby told her, 'this is a murder case and time is an important element in getting the facts straightened out.'

'I understand.'

'In order to solve questions such as motive and things like that, it's necessary to find out a great deal about a man's background.'

'I suppose so.'

'And, there's just a chance – a very good chance that Fred Albion Roff's presence in Madison City was connected in some way with this will contest case.'

'No comment.'

'That isn't going to help you any, Inez.'

'Thank you, I don't need help,' she said acidly.

'I think that you do.'

'I'd prefer to get licked standing on my own two feet than win by having Sylvia Martin go running around digging up evidence for me.'

'Perhaps you can dig up evidence for yourself.'

'Or have myself go running around digging up a story for her.'

'Why so bitter against her, Inez?'

'I'm not.'

'You sound like it.'

She said, 'Use your head, Doug. She's simply using you as a stalking horse to try and get a story.'

'I haven't seen her since …'

'Since when?'

'Since three o'clock this morning.'

'Your evenings,' Inez said coldly, 'seem to be *very* well occupied.'

Before Selby could reply, Judge Fairbanks emerged from chambers, nodded to the spectators to be seated, glanced over to make certain the jurors were all in their places and looked down at W Barclay Stanton. 'You have finished your opening statement, Counsellor?'

'I have hardly started, your Honour,' Stanton said, and twisted his lips in a smile as he waited for the laughter that he seemed to feel his wit merited.

Judge Fairbanks' tone was calmly impersonal. 'Proceed, then.'

Stanton looked at the unsmiling jury. Instantly, his tone assumed the orotund cadences of an orator who knows that he holds an audience which is unable to escape just as a scientist holds an impaled butterfly on a stout pin.

'And so, Ladies and Gentlemen,' he boomed, 'we come to a consideration of the sinister machinations of Martha Otley, the shrewd, designing adventuress, the scheming, unscrupulous, mercenary Judas, who masqueraded as the faithful employee, all the while she poisoned the mind of the testatrix with a long string of fabricated falsehoods that …'

'Just a moment, your Honour.'

Alphonse Baker Carr's voice had the reproachful quality of the man who rebukes one who has committed sacrilege within the sacred precincts of a chapel.

'Yes, Mr Carr. You wish to make an objection?'

'Yes, your Honour. It occurs to me that counsel should save his argument for the jury; that at this time he is only supposed to be making a preliminary statement setting forth the facts which he expects to prove, and this is hardly the time and hardly the place to malign a dead woman who has met her death in the employ of a woman whom she so faithfully served for so long a time.'

In the moment of tense silence which followed, Anita Eldon produced a dainty handkerchief, almost surreptitiously wiped a tear from her eyes, then sat perfectly still.

The effect was something as though Barclay Stanton had deliberately slapped her face.

Judge Fairbanks said, crisply, 'I think counsel will understand that in this preliminary statement counsel are only supposed to point out the facts which they expect to prove by the witnesses, so that the jurors can intelligently receive the evidence as it is presented. Argument will come later.'

W Barclay Stanton threw back his head, glowered across at A B Carr, and took a deep breath.

Selby slipped quietly out of the courtroom.

Out in the hallway, he found Sylvia Martin busily engaged in scribbling notes on a folded sheet of newsprint.

'Hello, Doug,' she said, looking up, and then dropping pencil and newsprint back into her purse. 'What do you think of the case?'

'I don't think,' Selby told her, laughing. 'I just this minute dropped in and heard a few of the preliminary pyrotechnics.'

'Doug, did you see what A B C's done to that girl?'

Selby nodded.

'You'd never know she was the same girl. She looks as pure as an Easter lily.'

Selby said, 'It occurs to me that we've all of us been inclined to underestimate Carr's talents. When you stop to think of it, it doesn't stand to reason that he would have been foolish enough to have walked into court in an agricultural community with a client who could have played the wicked woman vampire parts that are played in the motion pictures.'

Sylvia said, 'W Barclay Stanton isn't helping the case any. He's representing the brother, and he certainly takes himself seriously. But A B has a marvellous method of puncturing everything he does. Stanton pulls flamboyant grandiloquent stuff, and Carr lets all the wind out of it with just a word or two, or sometimes with just a gesture.'

'W Barclay Stanton is the kind who leads with his stomach. … Know something, Sylvia?'

'What?'

'I've been wondering. Since there was so much of a transformation in this Anita Eldon – well you know, she might be a pretty good actress.'

'What do you mean?'

'The description of that woman Coleman Dexter saw coming out of Roff's room – I'm just wondering if Anita Eldon might not have –'

'That woman was a brunette, Doug.'

'Well? Don't such things happen?'

'Yes. I suppose so, a transformation, a … Of course, Doug, he didn't get a good look at her.'

'I know. But suppose he took a good look at her now. She's an entirely different personality from what she was when we saw her yesterday. When she tries to look demure, she becomes self-effacing, and if she *did* happen to be the woman who was walking out of that room yesterday morning right after the murder, and was trying to appear self-effacing then – well, it just occurred to me there might be some resemblance.'

Sylvia Martin thought that over, then said, 'I wonder. You think we should get him down here to look her over, Doug?'

'It wouldn't be a bad idea to give him a ring and see if he could come down to the courthouse, slip in as a spectator, and look Carr's client over carefully. There's certainly a possibility she could have been the woman Coleman Dexter saw leaving that room.'

'Doug, I'm going to try it. What will we do? Telephone him? Or should we go to see him and explain …?'

Selby shook his head with a smile. '*We* shouldn't do anything, Sylvia. It's up to you. You see, I have no official status in the case and am only here as a visitor. I think that Carl Gifford somewhat resents my activities.'

'He would.'

'Well, you can't exactly blame him.'

'Bosh, Doug! You've got more brains in your little finger than he has in his whole body. He's a man who only goes through the motions of thinking. You resigned your office so you could enter the Army. He was glad enough to grab the district attorneyship so it would give him a good excuse … he …'

'Forget it,' Selby laughed. 'See if you can get Coleman Dexter and ask him to drop into the courtroom. What else is new – anything?'

She said, 'We've found out just a little more about Carr and his white gardenias.'

'What about them?'

'He had never met Anita Eldon. She was to have arrived from the East on the same train that you came in on, but at the last minute she changed her mind and decided to fly. Of course, her plane ticket took her through to Los Angeles, and she decided to stay there overnight and take the bus back to Madison City in the morning. She thought the bus would get in before the train did and she'd get in touch with Carr. But she overslept and missed the early bus and came in on the one that arrived a short time after the train was due. She telephoned Carr's house and found he was out – you see, Carr doesn't really have an office here. You know, Doug, if that house could talk, I'll bet it could tell plenty of stories. Anyhow, that's Anita Eldon's story. You see how it gives old A B C a clean bill of health.'

Selby nodded. 'What else have they found about Fred Albion Roff, anything?'

'Nothing much. That conversation with Inez Stapleton … I hate to play that up, Doug, but it's really the highlight in the story.'

'They've checked the hotel records to make sure that conversation *was* with Inez Stapleton.'

'With someone at her office number, and I guess there's no question but what she was in her office at the time.'

'What have they done about checking up with the hotel where he stayed in Los Angeles? Have they made any check to find out whether he received visitors or not?'

'I don't know, Doug. I haven't checked on that angle myself. I understand the Los Angeles police are working on it.'

Selby said, 'I'll go back and sit in the courtroom. You see if you can get Coleman Dexter to come down. Don't say anything to anyone else about it. And make it unofficial so that Carr won't get wise to it. If he knew what you were doing … Well, let's just keep it between ourselves.'

'I get you, Doug. You'll be here?'

'I'll be here.'

Selby went back to the courtroom.

Inez Stapleton was examining a witness who had apparently at one time been employed as a servant in the house. Inez was standing, slim and graceful, and Selby could see that she was commanding the attention of the jurors. Evidently, the rulings of Judge Fairbanks and the comments of A B Carr had choked W Barclay Stanton into at least temporary silence.

'Now, Mrs Dixon, please tell the jury exactly what you observed on that occasion.'

'You mean the time Mrs Otley prevented Miss Preston from writing the letter?'

Old A B Carr said, somewhat quizzically, 'Come, come, that's rather a conclusion of the witness that Miss Preston was prevented from writing a letter.'

Inez Stapleton whirled on him defiantly. 'That's exactly what we expect to prove.'

Carr's gesture was very magnanimous. 'Go right ahead and prove it, then, if you can. No one will welcome it more than I. I withdraw my comments. Your Honour, I was about to object to the statement made by the witness on the ground that it was a conclusion of the witness, but I shall withdraw it. By all means, let's hear how Miss Preston was *prevented* from writing the letter.'

'Go ahead,' Inez Stapleton said to the witness.

'Well, Miss Preston said she wanted to write a letter to her sister –'

'Now, by her sister, you mean Barbara Honcutt, the woman who is sitting over here at my left?'

'That's right. It was Mrs Honcutt.'

'Very well. And Miss Preston said she wanted to write a letter to her sister?'

'That's right.'

'And did Martha Otley do anything to prevent her from writing that letter?'

'Yes she did.'

'What?'

'Well, she went to get the fountain pen, and then she told Miss Preston that there wasn't any ink in the pen. But what she'd really done had been to go out and empty the pen down the sink so as to make certain it would be dry. And there wasn't anymore fountain pen ink in the house, and Miss Preston told her to get some fountain pen ink the next day, and that was all there was to it.'

Inez Stapleton glanced at the jury, saw that the jurors were listening attentively. She glanced at Carr and saw a slight smile twisting the corners of Carr's mouth.

'Now, I want to ask you about the time that Eleanor Preston wanted to go and visit her sister, Barbara Honcutt. What about that time?'

'Well, Miss Preston suggested that Martha Otley could get tickets and they'd go and visit her sister for three or four weeks and Martha Otley seemed sort of flabbergasted. She tried to think up something right quick, and then suddenly said, "You remember you've got an appointment with your dentist next week, and you'd better wait until after that tooth is fixed." '

'And then what happened?'

'And then Miss Preston said that was right, and well, that's the way it was, she didn't go.'

'You may cross-examine,' Inez Stapleton said, and sat down.

Old A B Carr ran his hand through the flowing locks of his hair. He stood up and regarded the witness for a minute or two in silent appraisal.

The witness was glowering at him belligerently, as though defying him to change her testimony by jot or tittle.

128

Old A B Carr smiled reassuringly at her, then walked halfway around the counsel table so that he stood where he could look directly at the witness. His manner was that of a benign friend merely helping a witness get her testimony straightened out.

'Reminded her that she had an appointment with her dentist?' he asked, conversationally, and with none of the manner of a cross-examiner.

'That's right.'

'Miss Preston *had* been having some trouble with her teeth?'

'Yes.'

'During the time that you were in her employ and while you saw Miss Preston and Mrs Otley together, you noticed those two occasions when Martha Otley had exercised undue influence over Miss Preston?'

And Carr held up his right hand with his two fingers extended in order to emphasize the number of two.

'Yes, sir.'

'That period covered how long a time?'

'About six months.'

'Did you like Mrs Otley?'

'She was all right.'

'Did you know Miss Preston's sister, Barbara Honcutt?'

'No.'

'Or her brother, Hervey Preston?'

'No.'

'Now naturally,' Carr said, 'as a fair-minded woman, when you saw Martha Otley attempting to influence Miss Preston in this way, you resented that, didn't you?'

'Well ... well, yes.'

'You weren't taken in any, were you?' asked Carr. 'You saw what Mrs Otley was trying to do. She didn't fool you any.'

'She certainly didn't! I sized her up the minute I clapped my eyes on her.'

'And, naturally, as an honourable, upright person, you resented her being there, and resented the undue influence she was bringing to bear on Miss Preston?'

'That's right.'

'So,' Carr said, as though that virtually disposed of the matter, 'you didn't like Martha Otley.'

'I didn't say that.'

Carr raised his eyebrows in surprise. 'You resented her attempts to influence Miss Preston?'

'That's right.'

'And you knew what she was trying to do?'

'Yes.'

'All along?'

'Well, yes.'

'Knew it as soon as you saw her, didn't you?'

'Well, I don't know what you mean by that.'

Carr's voice was patient. 'I understood you to say that you knew what was going on as soon as you clapped eyes on her.'

'Well, yes. I guess I did.'

'Now what was there at the moment that you first clapped your eyes on Mrs Otley that made you think she was trying to influence Miss Preston to make a will that would disinherit her brother and sister and leave her fortune to Martha Otley?'

'Well, you could just see it in everything she did.'

Carr held up his hand and motioned with his fingers as though he had been a traffic officer signalling to an automobile to back up. 'I'm talking now of the *minute* you clapped your eyes on her, Mrs Dixon. The *first* time you saw her.'

'Well … well, of course …'

'In other words, sort of an intuitive appreciation of her situation. Is that right?'

'Well, I guess so.'

'So, the minute you clapped your eyes on Martha Otley, you knew intuitively that she was trying to influence Miss Preston to disinherit her brother and sister.'

'Well, not quite that soon.'

'I don't want to misunderstand your testimony,' Carr said with the magnanimity of a man who is asking only what is fair. 'Now, I understood you to say you knew this the minute you clapped your eyes on Mrs Otley. If you *didn't* say that, please accept my apology. If you *did* say it, but didn't *mean* it, then let's change your testimony. Now, did you say that or didn't you?'

'Well … well … I guess I did.'

'But you didn't mean it? You now want to change your testimony?'

'No. I *did* mean it.'

'All right,' Carr said. 'Now we've got that one starting point definitely fixed in your testimony. The very first minute you clapped your eyes on Martha Otley you knew intuitively that she was trying to exert undue influence on Eleanor Preston. Now, because you're an upright, honest woman yourself, you resented that, didn't you?'

'Yes, I did.'

'And so, from the minute you clapped your eyes on Martha Otley there was an antagonism, a certain resentment.'

'All right, if you want it that way.'

'It's not the way *I* want it,' Carr said, turning to make a little inclusive gesture toward the *jurors*, 'it's the way the jurors want it. They want to know the facts, Mrs Dixon. They've got to find out the facts.'

'All right.'

'Your answer is yes?'

'Yes.'

'All right, *that's* settled. Now, during the six months that you were there in the house, there was nothing that changed your initial antagonism to Mrs Otley, was there?'

'Well, I don't know.'

Carr said, 'As I understand your testimony, Mrs Dixon, that initial resentment was brought about because of the fact that you knew the minute you clapped your eyes on Mrs Otley that she was trying to influence Eleanor Preston to make out a will that would disinherit her brother and sister. Now, if you changed in your feeling toward Mrs Otley, it must have been because subsequent events led you to believe that you had been mistaken in your initial appraisal.'

'Well they didn't. The more I saw of her, the more I knew I was right. Everything she did showed me I was right.'

'Therefore, you didn't *ever* change in your feeling toward her.'

'I'll say I didn't!'

'So, during all of the six months you were in the employ of Miss Preston and were in the house of Martha Otley, you felt a resentment toward Martha Otley? You called it a righteous resentment, but it was an antagonism, a definite resentment. Is that it?'

'Yes.'

'And I take it that Mrs Otley, being a woman of ordinary intelligence, soon discovered how you felt toward her.'

'Well, I guess she knew I didn't have any particular love for her.'

'So that made for a situation where there was some friction?'

'I don't know as I'd call it that.'

'Now then,' Carr said, smiling, 'as an upright, honest woman, and one who knew what Martha Otley's game was the minute you clapped your eyes on her, you decided that she wasn't going to get away with it if you could possibly help it, didn't you?'

'Yes, I did.'

'And so you kept your eyes open.'

'That's right.'

'For a period of six months?'

'Yes, sir.'

'And during all of that time,' Carr said, 'despite the fact that, right there, living in the house, you were watching every minute of the time with a firm determination to thwart Martha Otley in her purpose, you only saw these two instances of undue influence which you have just testified to.'

Once more Carr held his right hand high above his head, with the first and second fingers extended.

The witness hesitated.

'Only two instances in six months,' Carr said, moving his hand slightly as though to emphasize the rigidly upthrust fingers.

'Well, no, when you come right down to it, there were lots of things.'

'Then why not tell us about them?'

'I've forgotten about them.'

'Despite the fact that you made up your mind that you were going to thwart Martha Otley in her game, you have forgotten about them?'

'Well, they were little things.'

'And these two things were big things?'

'They certainly were.'

'Well, let's investigate those two things,' Carr said, smiling in the most friendly manner. 'Now, Miss Preston had some work done on her teeth.'

'Yes, sir.'

'Over a period of time?'

'A month or so.'

'She had some trouble with her teeth?'

'Naturally.'

'And she put off going to the dentist, didn't she?'

'Well, I don't know ...'

'Didn't you hear her complain about her teeth for a while before she went to a dentist?'

'Yes. She didn't want to go.'

'Exactly. And when she did decide to go, did she have some trouble getting an appointment?'

'Yes, she had to wait for three weeks in order to get her appointment.'

'So, she wasn't particularly anxious to go to the dentist, and when she did get an appointment, it took some little time. Now, Mrs Dixon, just to be fair, don't you think that if Martha Otley had wanted to use some undue influence to keep Eleanor Preston from visiting her sister, she could have thought up something better than an appointment with a dentist?'

'Well, that was what she thought up.'

'Are you sure that she *thought* it up?'

'Well, that's what you just said.'

'I may have suggested the idea to your mind,' Carr said, 'but the words were yours. That is, you agreed with me. Did she or did she not think it up?'

'Well, I suppose she did.'

'But there actually was an appointment with the dentist.'

'I believe there was.'

'So all that Martha Otley really did was to *remind* Miss Preston that she had an appointment with a dentist.'

'Yes.'

'You know that some people hire secretaries to remind them of their appointments?'

'I suppose so, yes.'

'And Martha Otley was really performing the work of a secretary?'

'She seemed to think she was.'

'So that when she reminded Miss Preston of a dental appointment, she was only doing what she was paid to do?'

'I don't look at it that way.'

'And on the occasion when she prevented Eleanor Preston from writing to her sister by telling her that the pen was dry, the pen actually was dry?'

'Naturally, after she'd dumped all of the ink down the sink.'

'And what sink was this that she spilled the ink down?'

'The set tub on the back porch.'

'And how did you know that she had dumped ink down there?'

'Because the next day I found some little drops of water that had ink in them on the side of the tub.'

'And there wasn't any more fountain pen ink in the house?'

'No.'

'And Miss Preston told Martha Otley to get some fountain pen ink the next day?'

'Yes.'

'And Martha Otley got it?'

'I believe she did.'

'And the fountain pen was then filled?'

'Yes, sir.'

'And there was nothing to have prevented Miss Preston from writing to her sister the next day?'

'She was probably out of the notion by that time.'

'She didn't say she was?'

'No.'

'She didn't say anything about it?'

'No.'

'But the fountain pen was there and she could have written to her sister?'

'I suppose so, yes.'

'Now, who filled the fountain pen?'

'I don't know.'

'And it was the next day that you found the drops of water on the side of the set tub?'

'Yes, sir.'

'After the fountain pen had been filled?' Carr asked.

'Well, I don't know whether it was before or after.'

'It may have been after?'

'Well, I don't think …'

'Do you know?'

'No.'

'Then it may have been after the fountain pen was filled?'

'Yes, I suppose so.'

'And there was inky water?'

'Yes, sir.'

'You knew it was ink?'

'Well, I think it was ink.'

'Now, if the fountain pen had been emptied down that set tub the day before, don't you think the water would have evaporated during the night?'

'I don't … I don't know. I don't think so.'

'But you don't know whether the inky water had been placed there that day or the day before?'

'Well, I guess not, when you come right down to it, I don't know.'

'You couldn't swear to it?'

'No.'

'So when Mrs Otley filled the fountain pen with ink she may have washed off the surplus ink in the set tub, or she might have spilled ink on her hands and washed that off in the set tub.'

'I suppose so.'

Carr smiled. 'And those were the only two things that you saw in six months of patient, careful observation while you were living right there in the house with these two women, with the firm determination that you were going to watch Martha Otley like a hawk in order to see that she didn't carry out this design of hers. Those were the only two things that you saw.'

'Well, they're the only two I can remember now.'

'And all the time you were there, from the minute you clapped your eyes on Martha Otley, you had a resentment for her?'

'I didn't say that.'

'I thought you did,' Carr said smiling, 'but after all, we'll leave that to the recollection of the jury. It's rather unimportant. The point is, Mrs Dixon, that for six months you lived in the house with these two women. You watched very carefully. You listened very carefully. You had a grim determination that you were going to thwart Martha Otley in her purpose. She wasn't going to slip anything over on you. You watched every move she made. You listened to every word she said, looking for some evidence that would show she was carrying out her purpose of unduly influencing Eleanor Preston. And yet, the only two instances that you saw were one instance when there was no fountain pen ink in the house, but Mrs Otley got some fountain pen ink and filled the fountain pen the next day, and the other instance was when she reminded Miss Preston of an actual appointment that she had with her dentist.'

The witness looked pathetically at Inez Stapleton for help.

'Do you understand that question?' Carr asked.

'I understand it the way you mean it.'

'Well, can you answer it?'

'Well, I don't think it's fair.'

'But those two instances were the only things you remember – if there'd been anything else you'd have told the lawyer for Barbara Honcutt about them? You'd have told the jury about them. Just those two things are all that you can remember?'

'Right now. Yes.'

Carr smiled and bowed. 'That's all, Mrs Dixon, and thank you for being very fair with us.'

Doug Selby turned toward the back of the courtroom, caught Sylvia Martin's eye. She was standing there with Coleman Dexter beside her.

'Your next witness?' Judge Fairbanks asked.

Carr said urbanely, 'Just for the sake of the record, your Honour, I want to state that as it now appears from the evidence this will was signed in my Los Angeles office. There were two subscribing witnesses present. One of these witnesses, a Mr Franklin L Dawson, has rather extensive business interests. He is here in court, and if the contestants wish to call him, he is available.

'The Court will remember that he has already testified in connection with the routine probate of the will. Now then, if the contestants desire to call him in connection with their claim of undue influence, Mr Dawson is available. If they do not wish to call him, however, I would like to have Mr Dawson excused from further attendance on the Court, as he is here at some considerable sacrifice to himself.'

'We're going to call him,' W Barclay Stanton boomed.

'Then he is available,' Carr said. 'Mr Dawson, will you take the stand please?'

'We don't need to call him right now,' Inez Stapleton interrupted.

Carr looked at her somewhat in surprise. 'I understand that Mr Stanton wanted to call him.'

'Put him on the stand,' Stanton bellowed. 'I'll examine him right now on behalf of contestant Hervey Preston, my client.'

'Very well,' Carr said.

Selby tiptoed toward the rear of the courtroom, nodded to Sylvia Martin. She and Coleman Dexter joined him in the corridor.

'Well?' Selby asked.

Dexter said, 'How are you, Mr Selby? My gosh, you wouldn't know that woman for the same woman seen yesterday coming out of that room, would you?'

'She's changed a good deal,' Selby said. 'I'm wondering if by any chance she's the woman you saw leaving Mr Roff's room yesterday morning.'

'That's what Miss Martin has been asking me,' Dexter said, 'and I hate to tell you folks the answer. The answer is that I just don't know. If you'd asked me yesterday if that blonde who had the room adjoining the room where the murder was committed was the one that I'd seen, I'd have told you there wasn't a chance in the world, but the way things are now I just don't know, Mr Selby, and I know that isn't doing you folks any good. I hate to appear dumb, but that's just the way it is.'

'You just can't tell?' Selby asked.

'To tell you the truth, I can't. There's been so much change in that woman between the time I saw her at the hotel yesterday and today that – well, to tell you the truth, Mr Selby, I'd have walked into court and sworn that I'd never in my life seen that woman before – the woman that's sitting there now, but I guess she's Anita Eldon, the same woman that I saw half a dozen times at the hotel and I sure looked her over then. The way she's changed her hair and something about her clothes and the way she wears them makes her look altogether different. She's like a sweet, demure little schoolgirl now, but when I saw her at the hotel yesterday, she was like a million dollars, conscious of her clothes and conscious of her hips. Sort of the kind that gets looked over and likes to be looked over, but will turn around and wither you with a haughty glance if they catch you looking them over. That's not a good description, but …'

Selby laughed. 'I think it's an excellent description, but the point is, *could* she have been this woman you saw coming out of the room?'

'I think she could, but I can't say that she was. That woman lawyer *could* have been the one. They're both the same build, slim, good figures and all that. Understand me, Major, I just turned around and gave that woman a glance. There wasn't any reason for me to look at her twice. She was just a woman with some laundry. It wasn't until afterwards I remembered about this paper lying there in the hall by my door. I don't know for sure whether I saw it just flutter as though it had just hit the floor, or what it was, but when I thought it over later, something gave me the impression that she'd dropped the paper, I just wasn't thinking about her. I had other things on my mind and I walked on down to my room, and that's all there is to it. I'm afraid that there's nothing I can do that's going to help except to swear that a woman came out of that room at that particular time, and that there were some clothes over her arm.'

'You knew that some woman came out of that particular room at that time?'

'I'll swear to that, Major Selby, and no lawyer on earth is going to shake me on that point. But when it comes to identifying that woman, to tell you the truth, I just wouldn't be any good at all. I've been listening to this man Carr in there, and – it doesn't make any difference who that woman was, I couldn't identify her, because, if I got on the stand and tried to identify any woman, that lawyer would tie me all up in knots and my testimony wouldn't be any good at all. As a matter of fact, that woman lawyer looks more like the woman I saw than the blonde. But I – I can't identify anyone.'

'But you could testify that *a* woman came out of that particular room at that particular time?'

'Mr Selby, a woman came out of that room at that time. She had some clothes over her arm. I *think* she dropped that paper that was in the hallway, but I can't swear to that. I can and will swear that a woman came out of that room and all the lawyers on earth can't change *that* testimony.'

'You know definitely that she came out of that particular room?'

'Out of that particular room.'

'It couldn't have been the adjoining room?'

'No, sir, it could not. She came out of that room. I saw her open the door. I saw her stand there for a minute and she looked sort of surprised as she saw me. I was bent over putting out that cigarette stub and when I looked up she was walking toward me, and I turned and walked on down the corridor.'

'And you didn't notice the paper lying on the carpet of the corridor when you first saw her.'

'I didn't, Major. The paper *may* have been there. I think she dropped it. That's another thing that I can't swear to. I can only say that I think she dropped it.'

'But you do remember now that there was a paper there on the floor when you looked up from putting out the cigarette and saw the woman coming?'

'I do, now, yes sir.'

'And you can fix the time?'

'I can fix the time absolutely, Major Selby. It was nine-fifty, and I'll swear that I'm not missing it by more than a minute either way ... Understand me, the things that I *know*, I'll swear to, but the things that I am not absolutely certain about, I don't want to try to swear to, because I'd just get up on the stand and some lawyer would make a monkey out of me.'

Selby said, 'That's just about all we can ask. I'm sorry we bothered you.'

'Not at all. I'm glad to do it, I'd like to help clear this thing up. Incidentally, I've closed the deal on that orange orchard and I'm going to be living here in the community, and I want to – well, you know, I want to do what's right.'

Sylvia Martin said, 'He was really busy this afternoon, Doug, but he dropped everything to come down here.'

Selby shook hands. 'Thanks a lot, Mr Dexter, I understand your position perfectly.'

When Dexter had gone, Selby turned to Sylvia Martin. 'It's a lot better to have a witness like that than one who will try to oblige you by saying the thing he thinks you want him to say and then get on the witness stand and go all to pieces.'

'Like that woman in there?' Sylvia asked laughing.

Selby said, 'It wasn't the woman as much as it was old A B Carr. You notice Carr played along with her until she made that statement that she knew what Martha Otley was up to as soon as she clapped her eyes on her. That was the pay off. From that minute, Carr had her right where he wanted her. He could come back to that any time he wanted to, and when he starts arguing to the jury he'll naturally claim that the witness was prejudiced against Martha Otley from the first time she saw the woman; that she reached the conclusion that Martha Otley was trying to get Eleanor Preston to disinherit her brother and sister, and that for six months she built up and nursed that insane prejudice.

'He'll ask the jury how anyone could possibly take one look at a woman and know intuitively that she was trying to get someone to make a will disinheriting her relatives.'

'And yet, it was such a natural thing for the woman to say,' Sylvia said. 'I didn't hear the first part of the cross-examination.'

Selby nodded. 'Those perfectly natural things we say are the things that betray us. Don't ever underestimate old A B Carr. If he hadn't trapped her on that, he'd have trapped her on something else. What do you say we take a run into Los Angeles and just check up for ourselves on the hotel where Fred Albion Roff stayed that night?'

Sylvia consulted her wristwatch. 'I'm working, Doug. I ...'

'It wouldn't take too long. We could be back by eleven o'clock, and, after all, this would be in the line of duty. We could have dinner and perhaps squeeze in a couple of dances during dinner, and ...'

'I'm just a poor spineless female,' Sylvia Martin protested, laughing. 'You've made a sale. Let me go telephone my paper.'

CHAPTER SIXTEEN

Selby and Sylvia Martin sat side by side in the bus that was bound for Los Angeles.

Her hand found his, squeezed it impetuously. 'Doug, it's so good to have you back.'

'It's good to be back.'

She waited a few moments then said, 'You're back, but still you're not back. I've just borrowed you for a while, just something that will make things a little easier – and a little harder.'

'What do you mean, Sylvia?'

'Easier while you're here, harder after you've gone. I miss you, Doug. Lots of people miss you. The County needs you. Are you coming back to the district attorney's office?'

'I don't know.'

'Of course,' she said, 'you're not really the old Doug Selby. You're bigger and broader. Why don't you want to come back and be district attorney, Doug?'

He turned to face her. 'I don't know, Sylvia. I want to work. I want to do the best I can with what I have.'

'To make more money?'

He shook his head impatiently. 'Making money doesn't appeal to me. I used to think of work in terms of money. Now I like to think of work in terms of accomplishment.'

'The Army, Doug?'

'Not the Army. The Army is only a means to an end.'

'What, then?'

'I don't know. We're entering an entirely new era.'

'But, Doug, there'll be peace and we'll have power. We'll have a Navy and airplanes and ...'

'And they won't do us a darn bit of good,' Selby said, 'unless we have definite principles and the will to fight to back up those principles. We've got to decide what we want and determine how we intend to get it. And we haven't much time to lose. While we're trying to make up our minds other nations will capitalize on our indecision by taking what they want and adding to their potential power at the same time they subtract from ours. I want to fit into something big, Sylvia. And the way to be a part of something big is to do a lot of small things well.'

'In Madison City?' she asked somewhat wistfully.

'It might be Madison City,' he told her. 'A nation is composed of cities, and the cities are composed of people, and the nation somehow has to be welded together. Lots of people in lots of cities will have to ...' He broke off and laughed. 'After all, we're getting into deep waters, but I may come back to Madison City. I may be a district attorney. I may be a judge. But whatever I am, I'm going to try to remember that every man in every job has to accept a new responsibility. Politicians must give way to statesmen. And always I want to remember that I can best take part in the big things by doing lots of little things well.'

'Such as finding out who murdered Fred Albion Roff?' she asked, half mischievously.

'Such as keeping a friend from being double-crossed by a political cut-throat,' Selby said. 'I'm not at all satisfied with the way Gifford is going about this thing. He's letting old A B Carr make up his mind for him, and when it comes to a showdown, if Carr makes a monkey out of the law enforcement officers, Gifford will blame everything onto the sheriff's office for failing to marshal enough evidence to enable him to get a conviction. And it will look perfectly plausible. There's enough circumstantial evidence to make the average man on the street feel that Farley really is guilty.'

'But, Doug, isn't that just one of the things that you can't avoid? I mean when you're in the position Rex Brandon is in, you're more or less at the mercy of the district attorney – in case he wants to give you a double-cross?'

'There's probably only one answer to it,' Selby said.

'What's that?'

'If Farley is guilty, get the evidence that will convict him. If he isn't guilty, find out who is guilty and prove Farley innocent by proving that someone else is guilty.'

'And you think Farley is innocent?'

'I don't know. I'm trying to find out.'

'When Carl Gifford realizes what you're doing, he won't like it.'

'Exactly.'

'Will that stop you from doing it?'

'No.'

'But you just said that you didn't want Gifford to think that you were horning in.'

Selby laughed and said, 'I'm trying to do what I do in such a way that I'll have it all done before there can be any criticism.'

'And they haven't enough evidence now to get a conviction?'

'Nowheres near enough. In order to prove a murder case, you nearly always have to prove a motive. In order to prove a motive, you have to know a great deal about the people with whom you're dealing. The murderer is alive. He's in a position to cover up. The dead man isn't. Therefore, the first principle in investigating a murder case is to find out every single thing you can about the corpse.'

'That's the way you used to play it, Doug?'

'That's the way Rex Brandon and I used to go about it,' Selby said, 'and I think it's a good way.'

Thereafter, they were silent for several minutes. Sylvia Martin looked out of the window, then closed her eyes, leaned her head back against the cushioned seat, said drowsily, 'These murder cases are hectic, but it's good to have you back, Doug,' and almost immediately fell asleep, her head naturally gravitating over until it rested against Doug Selby's shoulder.

From the bus depot in Los Angeles, they went directly to the Palm Vista Hotel. The Los Angeles police had been there before them, and the manager of the hotel was inclined to be uncommunicative. He had turned over all of his records, everything he had, to the police. There had been a long-distance call …

'Was it the only one?' Selby asked.

'It was the only one.'

'Did Roff receive any visitors in his room?'

The manager didn't know. He said somewhat indignantly that he couldn't be expected to know.

'Any local telephone calls?' Sylvia asked.

The record of that had also gone to the police. The manager believed there had been one call to a downtown hotel, but he wasn't certain.

Selby nudged Sylvia Martin. 'Well,' he announced, yawning prodigiously, 'I guess there's nothing to be done about it. We came in from Madison City and we're tired. How about vacancies?'

The manager referred him to the room clerk, who found that he had two singles, emphasizing very positively that they were on different floors.

Selby calmly registered and handed Sylvia Martin the pen. She registered, and Selby gravely took out a billfold. 'My baggage is coming along later,' he said. 'We'll pay in advance. Is there a good restaurant around here?'

The clerk glumly assured them that not only was there no good restaurant anywhere in the city: food was terrible, service awful, prices high. His manner was dyspeptically pessimistic as he handed Selby the change from a ten-dollar bill. There had been one or two very nice restaurants near the hotel, but they couldn't get help and when they did have help, they couldn't keep it. Then they couldn't get the food. Now you got things fried in rancid grease, burnt in too hot an oven, served without condiments, and prices were terrible. Selby went up in the elevator, said casually to Sylvia Martin, 'See you after a while,' and was shown to his room.

Selby enjoyed the luxury of a hot bath, then, in undershirt and trousers, telephoned for a bellboy.

The bellboy gave attentive consideration to Selby's request for two packs of one of the more popular brands of cigarettes, and a bottle of Scotch whisky.

'I can get 'em, but it's going to cost something.'

Selby agreed that one must necessarily pay for service, and after the commercial details had been concluded, finished dressing while he was waiting for the whisky, cigarettes, two glasses, two bottles of soda, and plenty of ice.

'*Two* glasses?' the bellboy commented blandly.

Selby met his eyes. 'Any reason why there shouldn't be two?'

'None that I know of.'

'How is this place – strict?'

'It doesn't like noise.'

'No noise, everything okay?'

'Everything's okay.'

'You on night before last?' Selby asked.

'Uh huh.'

'What is there the manager didn't want you to tell about Roff who was in nine-o-three?'

'I don't get you.'

'About the dame that called on him,' Selby said, carelessly. 'What was the idea?'

The bellboy hesitated a moment, then blurted, 'Well, since you know about it – oh, well, you know how it is. It might not look so good in the newspapers.'

'That the only visitor he had?'

'Far as I know she was. He'd had some hootch sent up before she came. Personally, I think it was on the up and up, but in the newspapers … well, you know, it was just one of those things that there wasn't any need to talk about. How did you know about it?'

'Oh I know her,' Selby said casually. 'She certainly is a darb, isn't she?'

'I'll say she's a darb – the real McCoy. She came breezing in just like she owned the place and got in the elevator and wanted the ninth floor. We knew she wasn't roomed here, and when a jane comes in and pulls that line, we make it a point to see where she's going. So we spotted her into nine-o-three and the manager told me to walk past the room a couple of times and see if there was any noise.'

'There wasn't?'

'No noise. She was a regular little lady – came out about an hour afterwards and went on about her business. Personally, I don't think she'd even had a drink. Don't say I spilled anything in case … well, you know how it is.'

'I know how it is,' Selby assured him and handed him another dollar.

When the bellboy had left, Selby gave Sylvia Martin a ring. 'Come on down and have a drink.'

'Is it all right, Doug?'

149

'It's all right, just so you don't make any noise. I have that assurance from headquarters.'

She laughed, said, 'I'll be quiet, but it will be five minutes.'

Selby opened the door when he heard her tap on the panels. He poured out drinks, splashed in soda water, smiled at her over the bubbling brim of the glass, and said, 'Here's to crime.'

'Here's to crime. Why do you have that expression of the cat that has just successfully looted the canary cage?'

Selby said, 'I was putting myself in Roff's position.'

'What does that have to do with it?'

'Well, you know if I were a lawyer who had uncovered something that might be pretty much worth while, and I started to peddle the information, I'd naturally want to peddle it to the highest bidder.'

'Well?' she asked.

Selby said, 'Roff came West on the train. That train went right through Madison City. He didn't get off. He went on to Los Angeles. He stayed here in this hotel. After he'd been here for a while, he called Madison City. Now, if he'd been wanting to talk with someone in Madison City on a matter of importance, he could have gone there *first*. When you're selling information to the highest bidder, you don't talk with only one bidder.'

'Doug, you mean you think he talked with old A B Carr?'

Selby said, 'I think he talked with Anita Eldon. I don't think he wanted to deal with another lawyer. I think he wanted to deal with clients first, and not with lawyers unless he had to.'

'But he called Inez Stapleton.'

'Because he had to. There were two clients on the other side. Inez Stapleton was the only one who was in a position to get them both together, but on the proponent's side on the case, there was only one – Anita Eldon.'

'Are you sure it was she?'

'No. I can only surmise it, and I lack the official power to make that identification absolute. I wish we had a photograph of her.'

'But I have, Doug.'

'You have?'

'Good heavens, yes. You didn't think the *Clarion* would let a million-dollar will contest come to trial with a beautiful blonde trying to climb aboard the gravy train and not have photographs?'

Selby's eyes were sharp with interest. 'A photograph of the blonde the way she was, or the way Carr had dressed her up?'

Sylvia laughed. 'That's once where old A B Carr slipped up. He forgot about the vanity of his client. She might be willing to appear in court as the demure, plain little girl who is dazed by the greedy world, but she wasn't going to have her photograph in the papers looking that way.'

'You have the picture with you?'

'Not the picture; but a proof we pulled.'

'Let's take a look at it.'

Sylvia took from her purse a folded sheet of newsprint some eight by ten inches, on which appeared reproductions of three photographs. In the centre was the glamorous, blonde beauty of Anita Eldon. On the left was old A B Carr in a pose that emphasized the strength of his clean-cut, thoughtful features. Over on the right was a photograph of Inez Stapleton and below the pictures was printed: '*Glamorous principal and opposing attorneys who are battling for million-dollar estate in the will contest which is now being tried in Superior Court here.*'

'I think that will do it,' Selby said, and holding the newsprint in his hand went to the telephone, asked for the bellboy, and was careful to specify that bellboy number four was the one who was to answer the call.

Selby opened the door as soon as he heard the boy's knock.

The bellboy regarded Sylvia Martin with the cynical appraisal of a man of the world who has no illusions whatever, then turned to Doug Selby, his manner expectant.

Selby said, 'I wonder if you'd recognize a picture of the woman who went to room nine-o-three the other night?'

'I could try,' the bellboy announced grinning. 'I darn seldom forget a pretty girl,' and favoured Sylvia with another glance.

Selby extended the sheet of newsprint with its three photographs, and its caption.

'That the one?' he asked.

The bellboy squinted his eyes thoughtfully, looked at the paper for some five or six seconds. 'That's the one,' he announced.

Selby's voice showed his excitement. 'You're positive?'

'Sure I'm positive. It's a good picture of her.'

'In other words,' Selby said, 'if it comes to a showdown you can swear absolutely that this woman,' tapping Anita Eldon's picture, 'went to the room that was rented by this man Roff ...'

'Hey, wait a minute. Which one are you talking about?' the bellboy asked.

Once more Selby tapped Anita Eldon's picture.

The bellboy shook his head. 'This is the broad that went up there,' he said, and placed his finger firmly and positively on the picture of Inez Stapleton.

CHAPTER SEVENTEEN

There was still a light in the window of Inez Stapleton's office. Selby climbed the stairs, and fatigue made his feet seem as heavy as his heart. He walked down the corridor, tried the outer door of the office and found it locked. He knocked, then after a moment knocked more loudly.

Steps sounded on the carpeted floor. A hand was on the knob on the inside of the door as though ready to unlock it. Then, apparently some uneasiness caused the hand to hesitate. Inez Stapleton's voice called out, 'Who is it?'

'It's Doug, Inez.'

'Are you alone?'

'Yes.'

She unlocked the door, let Selby in.

She looked thin and white. The skin under her eyes was dark with fatigue. Her features seemed pinched and drawn, but her head was back and her shoulders erect.

'I've been gathering a little legal ammunition,' she said, and her smile was merely a distortion of the lips. 'It's mostly duds.'

Selby said, 'I want to speak to you. I hate to talk to you when you're tired.'

'It's all right. I was just closing up and getting ready to go home.'

Selby said, 'It's after one.'

'I know it.'

Selby followed her into the inner office, took the seat which she indicated on the other side of the desk which was littered with law books. A pad of yellow foolscap showed the top sheet was filled with scribbled notes.

Selby's voice was kindly, but there was in it the beginning of a probing insistence. He said, 'Fred Albion Roff was murdered here at the Madison Hotel. He was in Los Angeles the night before he met his death. The records show that he telephoned you at your office.'

'That's not new, Doug.'

'It's preliminary.'

'To what?'

'Henry Farley is the waiter at the hotel who took the poisoned food up to the room. He has a criminal record. Some poison was found in his room.'

'Well?'

'A B Carr is defending him.'

'I know all those things, Doug.'

'And Carr rushed Gifford into filing a case against him. I understand that Carr is going to waive putting on any testimony at the preliminary and will contest that this man be bound over. That will mean that Gifford is virtually irrevocably embarked upon the prosecution of that waiter for first degree murder.'

'Well?'

'So far, Gifford hasn't been able to uncover any motive.'

'And what does all of that have to do with me?'

'It has to do with *me*,' Selby said. 'That's the thing I'm trying to tell you first. Rex Brandon is my friend. If the case against Farley blows up, it is quite possible that Gifford will bail out. He'll throw the blame on the sheriff's office for not having accomplished one single thing from the moment the district attorney's office filed its case.'

'That's just an assumption on your part?'

154

'Just an assumption,' he said. 'However, I think it's a logical assumption. I don't want it to happen. I want to find out more facts before Farley's preliminary takes place. I think you can tell me some of those facts.'

'No comment,' Inez said, her lips hardening so that little tired calliper lines came from the edges of her nostrils.

'I know,' Selby said, 'but there's something else that I have to tell you. Tonight I went to Los Angeles, trying to find some evidence.'

'Alone?' she asked and the question was almost taunting in its tone.

'Sylvia Martin went with me.'

'Out of friendship for Rex Brandon, I presume?' Inez said.

Selby didn't pay any attention to the comment. He said, 'We went to the hotel where Fred Albion Roff had stayed. I felt absolutely certain that he must have had something to do with this case. I thought that Anita Eldon might very well have called on him at his room there. I got one of the bellboys talking and showed him a picture of Anita Eldon. It was one of a group of pictures that the *Clarion* is going to run tomorrow morning. He picked out the photograph of the woman who had gone to Roff's room, all right, but the photograph wasn't that of Anita Eldon. It was a picture of you.'

The silence that followed Selby's statement lasted for what seemed an interminable interval. Selby was conscious of the stale air of the office after the fresh tang of the outer night. His nostrils were also conscious of that peculiar slightly acrid dust smell which is given off by old leather-backed law books that have long lain dormant.

'Well?' Selby asked.

Inez Stapleton tilted her chin even a little higher.

'No comment.'

155

'You can't get away with it, Inez,' Selby explained patiently. 'I didn't bring Sylvia with me because – well, because it didn't seem right.'

'Why wasn't it right?' Inez blazed at him. 'You might as well wear her around your neck! You've been here two days and I haven't seen you over thirty minutes. You've been running around …'

'What I'm getting at,' Selby interrupted, 'is that Sylvia Martin is working for a newspaper. She's a professional woman. She has a job to do. She's uncovered some news. She's going to have to publish it.'

'Let her publish it.'

'And when that happens, it means that old A B Carr, with that masterly timing of his, will adopt an air of hurt innocence. He'll let the impression get around that if Fred Albion Roff had lived, he would have blown your will contest case sky-high; that perhaps you didn't bring about his death, but that you were certainly in a position to profit by his murder, and that now you're trying to make hay while the sun shines. In order to accomplish that and win your will contest case, you're deliberately letting his client, Henry Farley, take the rap for a murder that could be cleared up if only you'd speak.'

Inez Stapleton's eyes were no longer tired. They were hard and defiant. 'No comment,' she spat at him.

Selby got up from his chair. He slowly walked around the desk. His left arm circled Inez Stapleton's shoulder. His right hand smoothed her forehead, ironing out the little wrinkles of tension and worry. 'Don't do it, Inez,' he pleaded. 'At least tell me. Let's see if we can't work something out.'

And then suddenly he realized that his fingertips which were touching her eyes were wet; that she had become limp and that tears were oozing out from under the tightly closed lids of her tired eyes. Her face twisted into a spasm of grief. She pushed his hands away, spread her arms on the desk, put her head down and sobbed.

Feeling awkwardly masculine and utterly futile to cope with this new mood, Selby patted her shoulder reassuringly for a second or two, then quietly moved over to a chair and let Inez cry it out.

It was nearly five minutes later that she raised tear-swollen eyes, wiped her face with a handkerchief, and said, 'All right. You win. I guess everyone wins, except me.'

'I'm not winning, Inez, I'm only trying to help.'

'Help whom?'

'You.'

'And Sylvia Martin and Rex Brandon.'

'All right,' he told her, 'I'm trying to help all of them. I'm trying to help my friends.'

'Doug, I can't talk.'

'Why not?'

'Because if I talk to anyone, it will appear in the paper. And if it appears in the paper, I've thrown what little chance my clients have to win this case out of the window.'

'Can't you talk to me?'

She shook her head. 'I'm a lawyer, Doug. I'm representing my clients.'

'If you *don't* talk, your case is going out of the window,' Selby said grimly.

'It's out of the window anyway. A B Carr, with his fatherly air of compassionate concern for his client, his grave, gentlemanly old-school gallantry for a damn little gold-digger, and W Barclay Stanton strutting around the courtroom stuffing his shirt full of W Barclay Stanton – Bosh! I'm sick of the whole business!'

'I think you'd better tell,' Selby said.

She shook her head. 'I can't. I won't. I'm damned if I do.'

'I think you should.'

'I won't.'

Selby said, 'I've got to tell Rex Brandon, Inez. The newspaper already knows. They'll call the Grand Jury in session. You'll be subpoenaed.'

'I have a right to a privileged communication.'

'From a client. Not from anyone else.'

'Doug, I can't tell what happened.'

'You've got to tell what happened.'

Suddenly she looked up with a flash of hope. 'Doug, do something for me.'

'What?'

'Come in this case.'

'What do you mean?'

'Associate yourself with me. Come in as one of the lawyers. Then I can talk to you. I can tell you the whole thing. It's an awful mess. You'll know what to do. I don't know. I'm groping in the dark. I can't talk to anyone because I can't betray the interests of my client. But if you were associated with me – look, Doug, I'll split the fee with you. I'll …'

He shook his head.

'No, I thought not,' she said wearily. 'You run around and help everybody else, but – '

'No splitting of the fee,' Selby interrupted with a smile. 'Pay me what I'm out of pocket on the case if you win, and I'll associate myself with you – at least until tomorrow afternoon when my furlough runs out.'

She was spilling the words at him almost before she realized the terms of his acceptance.

'Doug, this man telephoned me the night before last. He was a lawyer. He said that he wanted to discuss the case with me; that he might consider associating himself in the case with me; that he was from Kansas and he had some important new evidence that no one knew anything about; that he would go in it on a contingency basis; that he wouldn't charge a cent unless he could win the case hands down.

'I can't begin to tell you how low I was right then. I'd been working on the case. I realized that the law made it almost impossible to establish a case of undue influence in a will contest. It was necessary to show the undue influence right at the very moment of executing the will, and old A B C had his fine Italian hand in that. Well, you know how it was. My witnesses were beginning to get indefinite, and I saw what I was up against.'

Selby nodded.

'When someone comes to you to take a case, you listen to what they have to say and feel that they have a case, and think, "Oh, sure, things will work out as I begin to develop the evidence," and you go right ahead and are full of optimism. Then when you begin to prepare for trial, you realize that it's just the other way around; that your witnesses put their best foot forward when they talked with you the first time; that as they realize what they're up against, and know that Carr is going to cross-examine them, they begin to get more and more indefinite. And Carr, with that deft, sure touch of the absolute genius, manages to make everything come out all right for him. His side keeps getting stronger, and yours keeps getting weaker.'

'So you went in to see Roff?' Selby prompted.

'I talked with him for a little while over the telephone and he wanted to see me. I told him I'd see him the next day, and he said that wouldn't do – I had to see him right away if I wanted to do business; that otherwise it would be too late.'

'So you went in?'

'Yes, I had enough gasoline to make the trip. I jumped in my car and drove in. I left the lights on in my office while I was gone – just as a blind in case anyone was checking up on me.'

'And you saw him?'

'Yes.'

'What did he say?'

'Doug, it was the most awful thing I ever listened to in my life.'

'Go ahead.'

'He said that he had one course of action that would enable me to win the case; that he had the witnesses and everything; that on the other hand, he could throw the case the other way just by lifting his little finger. He said that he had a witness coming on the train the next day – he didn't mention who it was – who could either win or lose the case. He told me that if I made a deal with him he had something that was absolutely bulletproof; that I could win the case hands down but I could never win the case on my theory of undue influence, not with the witnesses I had. And then he came to the part that made me mad. He said he wanted fifty cents on the dollar.'

'You mean half of your fee?' Selby asked.

She said, 'Not half of my fee but half of everything in the estate. He said that he would take it in the form of a contract by which he would absolutely guarantee to win the case. But in return, he had to have that money paid to him as a fee, and he would take care of the witnesses and I gathered – well, at least one of the witnesses wanted to be paid, and another one was to be suppressed – sent out of the country. That was a witness who would swear that Eleanor hated her brother and sister and had said so before Martha Otley ever started working for her.'

'What did you do?'

'I told him there was absolutely nothing doing, and I thought he was just trying to chisel in on the case.'

'Then what?'

'Then he smiled and said that he had thought perhaps I'd adopt that attitude, but that he wanted to give me a chance. He said that he'd be in Madison City and that if I wanted to change

160

my mind before nine-thirty the next morning I could get in touch with him at the Madison Hotel; that after that it would be too late.'

'So what did you do?'

'I came back home.'

Selby said, 'Now let's get this straight, Inez, because it's important. Did you say anything to your client?'

'Yes. I told her about it.'

'You mean Barbara Honcutt?'

'Yes.'

'When?'

'About eight o'clock the next morning I telephoned her at the hotel.'

'Why did you tell her and what did you tell her?'

'I told her exactly what had happened and exactly what I had done. I told her I thought the man was a chiseller; that I didn't like the idea of suppressing evidence and I didn't like the idea of blackmail, even when it was put up in that form.'

'And your client agreed with you?'

'Yes.'

'Did she say anything to her brother?'

'I think she did.'

'And to W Barclay Stanton?'

'Heavens, I hope not.'

'But you don't know whether or not they said anything to him?'

'No.'

'Did you see Fred Albion Roff after he came to Madison City?'

'No.'

'Did you try to?'

'No. I made up my mind I'd paddle my own canoe. I didn't want to be mixed up in the case with that type of lawyer.'

161

'And why didn't you tell Rex Brandon about what had happened?'

'Doug, don't you see? Can't you see? Then I'd have had to tell the whole story, that a witness would swear Eleanor had hated her brother and sister. A witness who must have come to Madison City on that train. You remember that Roff telephoned down to find out if the train was on time. If I say anything, it will give Carr all the information he needs to hunt up that witness, and then what little chance I stand of winning the case will be absolutely lost.'

'What happened in court this afternoon?' Selby asked. 'After the afternoon recess?'

She said, 'Nothing much. They put one of the subscribing witnesses on the stand – or rather, W Barclay Stanton did. Any witness we don't call is deemed to be one who would have testified against us. That's the presumption under the law and – well, after all, when you're fighting a desperate case, you clutch at straws. We just went fishing, trying to find something that would help.'

'What happened?'

'This witness, Franklin L Dawson, went on the witness stand. He made a terrific impression. He told about Eleanor Preston coming in there to sign the will, about how she said to Martha Otley, "Now you stay right out here. I don't want you anywheres around when I sign this because that brother and sister of mine are apt to try and make trouble if they see my money slipping through their greedy fingers." '

'Then what?'

'Then she went into Carr's office and signed the will, and Carr wanted witnesses. One of them was his secretary, and the other one was this Franklin L Dawson who was waiting in the office to see Carr about another matter, and Carr called him in and asked him to witness the will. So he went in and of course swears that Eleanor Preston was absolutely normal, in her right mind, and in full possession of her faculties, and said that she wanted him to execute the will as a witness.'

'Anything else?'

'Oh,' she said, 'W Barclay Stanton ranted and raved around the courtroom and every time he opened his mouth he put his foot in it, until finally even the jury got to laughing at him.'

'And the witness was excused?'

'No. I'm supposed to question him when court opens in the morning ... I don't suppose there's anything you can do, but Stanton insisted we had to take a chance on these subscribing witnesses. Otherwise they'd claim we were relying on circumstantial evidence as to the things that influenced the testatrix at the time the will was executed, and failing to put on the best evidence – the subscribing witnesses. What *I* was trying to do was to show that Martha Otley accompanied Eleanor Preston to Carr's office and was with her right up to the minute she signed the will.'

Selby pushed back from the desk, got up and paced the floor. 'You've got to tell about that interview with Roff,' he said.

'But you can see what will happen.'

'If you don't,' Selby went on, 'it's going to come out anyway. It isn't a privileged communication. It didn't consist of anything your client said to you. It consisted of something that was said to you by Fred Albion Roff, and it *may* furnish a motive for his murder.'

'Sure,' she said. 'Leave it to old A B C. He'll make it appear that I told my client, and that she went right out and murdered the man and ...'

'That part,' Selby said, 'is something you *can* sit tight on. You don't have to tell them that you told your client.'

'I may not have to tell them that, but Carr will tell them for me. And Carr will probably dig up this witness and ...'

'Don't be too sure there is any witness, Inez.'

'What do you mean, Doug?'

'I mean Roff was in a dangerous position. He didn't dare to put his proposition boldly and truthfully because you might find out what he had in mind. He may have had two witnesses, or he may have had only one witness. Personally, I think he had just one witness, a woman. The man who was also on the train was a stooge, someone to keep a line on the witness. He was probably sent along to be sure she didn't leave the train at any intermediate stop. That's why he travelled by day coach. In that way he could get off at every stop – to watch the Pullman car where the woman was riding – making certain she didn't take a powder.'

'Doug, what are you talking about?'

'But,' Selby went on, 'Roff evidently had some theory by which he thought he could win the case; otherwise he wouldn't have made you such an offer.'

'Sure – by suppressing the evidence of a witness.'

'You can't win a will contest merely by *suppressing* evidence. He had something that was hot enough so he came all the way out here from Kansas, something that caused him to – let's think the thing over pretty carefully, Inez. We've got to put ourselves into the mind of a dead man and reconstruct his thoughts. Then we've got to find out the *method* by which he expected to win his case.'

'But what are we going to do first?'

'First,' Selby said determinedly, 'whether you like it or not, we're going to notify Rex Brandon of exactly what happened.'

'And Sylvia Martin?' she asked.

Selby met her eyes. 'You're going to give Sylvia Martin an exclusive interview,' he said. 'Remember, I'm associated in the case now.'

And Selby calmly picked up the receiver and dialled a number.

CHAPTER EIGHTEEN

The courtroom was hushed with an atmosphere of tense expectation. The *Clarion's* story of Inez Stapleton's connection with the murdered man, and her sudden trip to Los Angeles to see him had created a profound impression.

Judge Fairbanks ascended the bench, and court was called to order amid a silence of sheer tension. There was no whispering because spectators were afraid to take their eyes from the actors in the courtroom drama long enough to make even a whispered comment.

Inez Stapleton arose and said, 'Your Honour, I move at this time to associate Major Douglas Selby as one of counsel for the contestant, Barbara Honcutt.'

'Any objection?' Judge Fairbanks asked, as a matter of perfunctory courtesy.

Carr, all smiles, was on his feet. 'No, your Honour, not in the least. In fact, I may say, off the record, but for the record, that it is a pleasure to have so distinguished and able an opponent.'

Selby bowed and smiled, and Carr returned his bow with an air of grave sincerity.

'Franklin L Dawson was on the stand,' Judge Fairbanks said, 'and I believe you were about to examine him, Miss Stapleton?'

'Mr Selby will examine him,' Inez said.

'Very well. Take the stand,' Judge Fairbanks said to Dawson. Dawson, a tall, heavy-boned individual with high cheekbones, a long, firm mouth, and an air of rugged sincerity, adjusted himself on the witness stand.

'As I understand your testimony of yesterday,' Selby said, 'you were in Mr Carr's office at the time Eleanor Preston and Martha Otley entered.'

'That's right.'

'You had been there for some time?'

'Four or five minutes.'

'Did you have an appointment with Mr Carr?'

'I don't see what that has to do with it,' the witness said.

'I think I'm entitled to know all of the surrounding facts. Besides, it may be important,' Selby pointed out.

Carr smiled, waved a gracious hand. 'No objection, your Honour. None whatever. Let the witness answer the question.'

'Yes, I had an appointment with him.'

'Made over the telephone?'

'Yes.'

'Do you remember what time it was, then, when you entered his office?'

'Around three o'clock in the afternoon.'

'And what time was your appointment?'

'For three o'clock.'

'And Eleanor Preston and Martha Otley were there when you came in?'

'No, they came in later. I told you that before.'

'That's right. So you did. About five minutes later, would you say?'

'Yes.'

'So your appointment was for three o'clock, you arrived at three o'clock, and about five minutes later were still seated in Mr Carr's outer office – the reception room?'

'I guess so. I guess that's right.'

'And then these two women came in and sat down?'

'Yes.'

'Close together?'

'Side by side, I believe, on a settee at the far end of the room.'

'You couldn't hear their conversation then?'

'No.'

'Yet, as I understand it, you have testified that Eleanor Preston told Martha Otley to wait there in the office; that she didn't want her in the inner office when she signed the will.'

'I certainly did. She said her relatives had greedy fingers and would clutch at any straw.'

'You heard that?'

'Yes.'

'Heard that very distinctly?'

'Yes.'

'But you didn't hear any of the *other* conversation?'

'Not that I can remember.'

'How did it happen that you heard this particular bit of conversation? Did Eleanor Preston raise her voice so that you could hear it?'

'I guess she must have. I heard it.'

'And they were both sitting close together when Eleanor Preston made that statement?'

The witness shifted his position, glanced at Carr, said, 'I think Eleanor Preston was standing up.'

'And how about Martha Otley? Was she standing up or sitting down?'

'She was ... I guess she was sitting down.'

'So Miss Preston got up to deliver herself of that statement, at the same time that she raised her voice so that you could hear what she said?'

'Not exactly.'

'Now where was she standing, right by the side of this settee on which Martha Otley was seated?'

'No, she was in the door of Carr's office then.'

'But weren't you all three in Carr's office?'

'I mean Carr's private office.'

'Oh, then Mr Carr must have opened the door of the office.'

The witness coughed, glanced at Carr again, then said, 'I guess he did, yes, sir.'

'And Miss Preston was then standing in the door of the office?'

'Yes.'

'And Martha Otley was seated?'

'That's right.'

The witness began to show signs of restlessness.

'In the same position she had taken on the settee when the two women had first entered the office?'

'Yes.'

'Then there was no occasion for Miss Preston to raise her voice and advise Martha Otley to remain where she was, was there?'

'What do you mean by that?'

'Martha Otley hadn't made any attempt to follow her into Carr's private office, had she?'

'Of course, your Honour,' Carr said suavely, 'I want to give counsel the utmost latitude in this matter. We welcome having all the facts brought to light, but it occurs to me that this is, after all, something of an attempt to cross-examine his own witness.'

'The Court thinks the examination perfectly in order,' Judge Fairbanks said. 'The witness is obviously hostile and was called largely as a matter of necessity. Proceed with your questions.'

'How about it?' Selby asked, smiling. 'Did Martha Otley make any attempt to follow?'

'Well, I guess she would have.'

Selby's smile broadened. 'We don't want to know what you guess, and we don't want to know what you think Mrs Otley might have done under certain circumstances. What I am interested in finding out is whether Martha Otley actually did make any attempt to follow Eleanor Preston into Mr Carr's private office.'

'Well, no, I guess she didn't.'

'So then, this remark of Eleanor Preston's which was conveniently made in a tone of voice loud enough for you to hear, was uncalled for so far as any of the circumstances were concerned.'

'Objected to,' Carr said, 'as calling for a conclusion of the witness.'

'I will sustain the objection on that ground,' Judge Fairbanks ruled. 'The facts are before the jury, and the conclusion is for them.'

'But,' Selby persisted, 'you are positive that Eleanor Preston told Martha Otley not to try to follow her into Carr's private office?'

'Yes, sir.'

'And that up to the time that statement had been made, Martha Otley had made no attempt to follow her into the office?'

'Well, no, I guess not.'

'But had sat perfectly still.'

'Yes, sir.'

'So that that purely gratuitous remark which was made in such a loud voice that you could hear it, was made *after* Eleanor Preston had gone to the door of Carr's office, after she had turned around, and after she had seen that Martha Otley was still seated in the same position on the settee.'

'Yes, sir.'

'Didn't that impress you as being rather incongruous at the time? Don't you think, in searching your recollection, that there was perhaps some error there? Don't you think that a remark so obviously uncalled for would have impressed you as being utterly unnecessary?'

'That, of course, is argumentative,' Carr said.

'I'll stipulate that it is,' Selby said. 'I'm merely pointing out to the witness an inconsistency in his testimony and asking him if he can explain it.'

'No inconsistency,' Carr snapped. 'It's the same thing he has said all along.'

'It's an inconsistency with the facts,' Selby observed.

Judge Fairbanks said, 'Counsel will reserve their argument for the jury, but I will let counsel point out to the witness the fact of any seeming discrepancy between the facts as he has testified to them and his recollection of the conversation.'

'Well, if I've got to tell *all* that happened,' the witness blurted, 'at first they both went into Carr's office, and then after a minute or two, Martha Otley came out and went back to where she'd been sitting on the settee, and *then* Eleanor Preston came to the door and told her not to try to be in the office with her when she signed the will.'

Selby smiled.

'So that Martha Otley had already gone into the office and *tried to be present when the will was being signed*?'

'Well, I don't know about that.'

'But she did go into the office with Miss Preston?'

'Yes – the first time.'

'And then she returned?'

'Yes.'

'And then, *after* she had resumed her position on the settee, Eleanor Preston stood in the doorway of Carr's private office and made this little speech to her.'

'I guess that's right, yes.'

'Talking clear across the office?'

'Clear across the office.'

'And Mr Carr was standing beside her in the doorway?'

'Yes.'

'And at the time she told Martha Otley not to follow her, Martha Otley had already tried to follow her, actually had followed her, and had been sent back, and was then sitting on the settee?'

'Yes, sir.'

'So that this little speech of Eleanor Preston's could very well have been made at the suggestion of our esteemed contemporary, the Honourable A B Carr?'

'I object, your Honour,' Carr said in a tone of wounded dignity, but his objection was drowned in laughter from the courtroom.

Judge Fairbanks frowned at Selby. 'I think, Major Selby,' he said, 'we'll leave those conclusions for the jury to draw.'

'Very well, your Honour,' Selby said, and then turned to the witness.

'Now, right *after* this speech had been made, Mr Carr invited you into the office to witness the execution of this will?'

'Well, yes.'

'And you did so witness the execution?'

'Yes.'

'In the presence of Mr Carr's secretary, who was the other witness?'

'That's right.'

'And in the presence of Miss Preston?'

'Yes, sir.'

'And then what did you do?'

'I went out.'

'Out of Carr's private office and back to the outer office?'

'Yes, sir.'

'And out of there to the street?'

'Yes, sir.'

Selby said with some surprise, 'I thought you had an appointment with Mr Carr?'

171

'I did.'

'On a business matter?'

'Well, Mr Carr asked me to drop in.'

'When had that conversation taken place?'

'The afternoon before.'

'So Mr Carr asked you to drop in?'

'Yes, sir.'

'Did he say why?'

'Well ... he said I'd be doing him a favour if I, well ... He said he'd like to have me come in. He wanted to – he asked me to come.'

'Indeed, yes. And you were under some obligation to Mr Carr?'

'What do you mean by that?'

'You owed him money, perhaps for a fee?'

'Yes.'

'He had performed some legal services for you?'

'Yes.'

'What was the nature of those services?'

'Your Honour, I object,' Carr said. 'This is absolutely and utterly incompetent, irrelevant, and immaterial.'

'It goes to show the bias of the witness,' Selby pointed out.

Judge Fairbanks said, 'I think I will sustain the objection as to the *exact* nature of the services.'

'Generally,' Selby asked, 'had Mr Carr been your attorney when you were accused of a crime?'

'Your Honour,' Carr protested in a pained voice, 'I renew my objection. I ...'

'Sustained.'

'So,' Selby said, 'Carr invited you to come to his office for the sole and specific purpose of being a witness to that will, so that in the event of a contest you could get on the witness stand and testify just as you are now testifying.'

'That also is a conclusion of the witness,' Carr objected. 'And I may state, your Honour, that I consider this examination most unfair.'

'It may be a conclusion of the witness,' Judge Fairbanks said, 'but counsel can reach it in another way.'

'Thank you, your Honour, I will,' Selby said. 'Did you have any business which you discussed with Mr Carr at the time you went to his office that afternoon?'

'Well ... I ...'

'Yes or no.'

'No.'

'You entered the office with a three o'clock appointment. You waited until about five minutes past three until two women came in. You made no objection when those women were received in Carr's private office ahead of you at a time when you had an appointment. You waited until Mr Carr called you, then you went in and executed the attestation clause of the will as a witness and then you went out. Is that right?'

'Well, I guess so, yes.'

'And Miss Eleanor Preston was still in Carr's office when you went out?'

'Yes.'

'And Martha Otley was seated in the outer office?'

'Yes.'

'And there was no other business which you had to transact with Mr Carr that afternoon?'

'No.'

Selby smiled. 'I think that is all.'

Dawson, running his hand over his perspiring forehead, scrambled from the witness stand with eager alacrity.

'Of course, your Honour,' Carr said, 'I protest that the examination of this witness was handled in such a way, a shrewd, skilful way, if you wish, but nevertheless in such a way it was made to seem that this witness had been accused of a crime. I think the jury should be admonished that counsel had no right to ask that question and that the jury are not to consider it as evidence.'

Judge Fairbanks said, 'I ruled the question out. Of course the witness cannot be impeached by showing he was accused of crime. But when it comes to showing bias I am not so certain ...'

'But your Honour,' Carr protested, 'that's the very crux of the matter. Counsel has ...'

Judge Fairbanks cut him off. 'I think, Mr Carr, that any obligations of the witness to counsel may be irrelevant. I ...'

The judge looked up as a commotion in the back of the courtroom caused him to frown.

For a moment there was a swirling among the spectators who were standing in the back of the courtroom, and then Sheriff Brandon came pushing through, and there was that in his manner which caused proceedings to come to a halt. Even Judge Fairbanks, pausing in mid-sentence, watched in silence as the sheriff proceeded with set fixity of purpose to the bar where Selby was sitting.

The sheriff bent over Doug Selby. 'Can you get out of here, Doug?'

'What is it?' Selby whispered.

'That little old woman, Mrs Irwin, the one with the flower.'

'What about her?'

'She's been poisoned.'

Selby was on his feet beside Rex, unconscious of the fact that every eye in the courtroom was fixed on them.

'Serious?' he asked. 'Fatally?'

'No, it's arsenic. Her stomach's been pumped out and I think she's going to make it all right. Can you get a continuance or get away from here somehow?'

Selby reached a sudden decision. 'Sit down, Rex, I'll be with you in a minute.'

Selby turned to address the court. 'May it please the Court. I have just learned that there has been another poisoning case at the Madison Hotel. The sheriff asked me to accompany him. Might I ask for a brief continuance, perhaps an hour or so.'

Carr said suavely, 'Your Honour, I dislike to object, but after all, Major Selby's connection with the County is no longer official. It's merely a matter of friendship for the sheriff. In the meantime, the rights of my client ...' here Carr paused to bend deferentially over the demure Anita Eldon, 'certainly are entitled to some consideration.'

Judge Fairbanks nodded.

'In that event,' Selby said in a ringing clear voice, 'the next witness for the contestants will be Hattie M Irwin.'

'Is Mrs Irwin in court?' asked Judge Fairbanks.

'Unfortunately she is not,' Selby said. 'She is a witness for the contestants and I understand that she has been poisoned.'

The reaction of the spectators was a collective gasp of startled surprise.

'Your Honour,' Carr thundered, 'I resent that. I resent the imputation. I resent the manner in which counsel has presented that to the court.'

Selby said, 'I am stating facts.'

'You have no right to state such facts.'

Selby said, 'I want Hattie M Irwin to take the stand.'

'Was Mrs Irwin subpoenaed by you?' Carr asked.

'She was.'

Carr couldn't conceal his surprise. 'When?' he asked, and the question was almost an ejaculation of incredulity.

'At approximately seven-fifteen this morning,' Selby said.

The courtroom was silent, watching the battle of wits between these two men – Carr feeling his way, a past-master in the art of ring generalship, Selby, fighting mad, belligerently insistent.

'As I understand it,' Carr said, 'under those circumstances, counsel may make a motion for continuance, and, as a part of that motion, may state what he expects the witness to swear to. Then the other side has the option of stipulating that if the witness were called she would so testify.'

Selby took the bull by the horns. 'I can't state what this witness would testify to,' he said, 'because I don't know.'

'You don't know?' Carr asked with just the right expression of profound surprise. 'Then why on earth did you subpoena her?'

'Since you've asked the question,' Selby said, 'I'll answer it. I subpoenaed her because I know that she knows something that is such a vital fact in this case that someone has tried to seal her lips by administering poison – and I want to find out what it is before she dies.'

'I object,' Carr roared. 'I cite that as prejudicial misconduct.'

'You asked me a question and I answered it. Stand up there and ask me some more questions and I'll answer them.'

'Gentlemen! Gentlemen!' Judge Fairbanks said. 'This is neither the time nor the place for an altercation such as this. Do I understand that the witness who is incapacitated has been subpoenaed by the contestants, but that the contestants are not in a position to state what they expect her to testify to?'

'That is correct.'

'Over the objection of counsel,' Judge Fairbanks said, 'I hardly feel that a continuance should be granted under those circumstances. The Court will, however, take a fifteen-minute recess, during which it is possible that some agreement may be reached by counsel. Court will take a fifteen-minute recess.'

Selby gave hasty instructions to Inez Stapleton. 'Keep away from Carr. Don't let him pump you. The Court probably won't grant the continuance. Put your next witness on the stand. Do the best you can with him. Just stall for time. I'm going to rush out there and see if I can find out what she knows.'

'You think she knows something, Doug?'

'You bet she knows something,' Selby said, 'and I'm going to find out what it is.'

CHAPTER NINETEEN

At the hospital, a nurse summoned Dr Thurman. The physician's face was stamped with the fatigue of overwork, long hours, grave responsibilities. His face had once been grooved into kindly lines of benevolence, the heritage of more carefree days when he had been able to find the leisure to take an occasional vacation or have an uninterrupted night's sleep. Now, his eyelids fluttered slightly as he opened and closed his eyes, and there was a slightly greyish pallor about the skin. There were pouches under his eyes and lines around his mouth.

'She's weak,' he said. 'She's out of danger, unless her heart gives out. But you can't go on any fishing excursions, gentlemen. If you have specific questions to ask, she can answer one question or perhaps two. No more.'

'How did it happen?' Selby asked.

'Don't know,' the doctor said. 'Arsenic was ingested in food she ate at the hotel. I've traced it to the sugar she put in her coffee. There was a sugar bowl on the table. There was arsenic sprinkled on the top of that sugar. She had been assigned a regular table in the hotel dining-room, a small table for two over near the window. Any person who wanted her out of the way only needed to put arsenic in her sugar bowl to be reasonably certain she would get it.'

'Provided, of course, he had access to the dining-room,' Selby said.

'It's a public place,' the doctor pointed out.

'But a transient would hardly have had the chance to put arsenic in a sugar bowl that a regular tenant or a waiter would have had. The tables for regular roomers are off to one side.'

'That's so, yes.'

'You found out what the poison was rather quickly?'

'Fortunately the symptoms were typical. I made a correct diagnosis almost immediately and got a stomach pump to work.'

'You saved the contents of the stomach for analysis?'

'Oh, sure.'

'She's weak?'

'Yes.'

'Frightened?'

'No. She has no idea a metallic poison was administered. She thinks it's just a case of ordinary food poisoning.'

'You'll tell her the truth before she leaves the hospital?'

'Certainly. She's entitled to know – when she's strong enough.'

'Can we ask her one or two questions now?' asked Brandon.

'Whenever you want. I'll go in with you myself or have the nurse take you in.'

Brandon said, 'Well, let's go, and ...'

Selby said, 'Wait a minute, Rex. Let's think. If we're limited to one or two questions, we are going to have to make those questions count.'

'Naturally,' Dr Thurman said, dryly.

'Has she said anything to you?' Selby asked. 'Anything that would give you any hint?'

'Not a thing. She keeps talking about some contest she won, and she's afraid she's going to get cheated out of the trip which was supposed to be first prize.'

Selby nodded. 'I know all about that.'

Selby said to Rex Brandon, 'Let's look at the thing this way, Rex. Fred Albion Roff came out here from Empalma. He arranged to have this witness come out here. He must have had an ace in the hole, a trump card that he could play, something that would enable him absolutely to *guarantee* a verdict in favour of the contestants in that will case.'

'That's what he *said*,' Brandon observed.

'It's what he said, and it's what he himself believed,' Selby said. 'He pushed his own stack of blue chips into the centre of the table on that assumption. He was a crooked lawyer. But he was no fool. He knew evidence and he knew law. He paid his own expenses out here. He evidently paid the expenses of this witness and of a man to see she didn't get off the train en route. The man took the day coaches so he could watch the Pullman at each stop. That must have been because the woman was his star witness. He bought her a Pullman berth. Roff had to assure himself that *she* would arrive in good condition. All that business about the contest was, of course, just an excuse, a subterfuge by which the man could get Hattie Irwin to arrive in Madison City at a certain date without letting her have the slightest idea of why she was being sent here. He arranged that so-called "contest" which consisted of one single letter sent to one person who naturally would be notified she had won the first prize – a trip to California. He probably knew she had acquired the habit of trying her hand at mail order contests. You can see he laid his plans carefully and thoroughly. He couldn't afford to have any slip-up. Therefore when he said he could *guarantee* a verdict in that will case he *must* have known what he was talking about. A lawyer smart enough to have arranged all that couldn't have been merely guessing. He must have *known*.'

'You're making a lot of deductions,' Brandon said.

Selby nodded and observed simply, 'We've got to, Rex. The murderer put the seal of silence on the lips of Roff and now he's tried to seal the lips of Hattie Irwin. We've got to break that seal.'

'All right. Keep talking,' Brandon said. 'As far as I'm concerned, you're doing fine.'

Selby said, 'I'm making a guess, Rex, that the man was a stooge, a guard, a sort of chaperon. The woman was the one Roff really wanted. She must be the one who has the really valuable piece of information, the thing on which Roff was willing to stake his big gamble. Roff was making an investment, and he wanted to keep that investment as low as possible, but he took every safeguard to see that Hattie Irwin travelled in comfort.'

'All right. I'll agree with you that far, Doug.'

Dr Thurman's eyes were sparkling with interest now. He said, 'I have never before realized just how you lawyers had to parallel our reasoning in making a diagnosis.'

Selby said, 'We have here a will contest. The principal ground of contest is undue influence. At the time of making the will, old A B Carr had the stage all set with that shrewd mind of his –'

'That crooked, unscrupulous mind of his,' Brandon interrupted.

'All right, have it that way if you want, but whether it's crooked or unscrupulous or whether it isn't, you must admit that it's shrewd. He carefully set the stage, knowing that there would be a contest of the will, and feathering his own nest so that he could be assured of winning that contest and making the will stand up.

'Eleanor Preston was a wealthy and an influential woman here in Madison City. She heard about Carr's skill and went to his office to have her will drawn, or perhaps it was Martha Otley who consulted Carr. Yes, it was probably Martha Otley who told Carr she wanted an absolutely bomb-proof will drawn up. Now, what single legal fact could absolutely throw that will out of court?'

'That's a legal question,' Brandon said. 'You've got to answer it.'

181

'Something in the execution of the will itself?' Dr Thurman suggested.

'Ordinarily, you would say that would be the answer. But the will was executed in Carr's office. There were two witnesses who were under Carr's domination. The most we've been able to show is that the affair was stage-managed by Carr's agile brain. But that isn't going to affect the execution of the will. It only contributes something to the question of undue influence. Moreover, Hattie Irwin had never been out of Kansas, at least during the period in question. She knows none of the parties.'

'All right, then that's out,' Brandon said.

'Now then, what else could there be – nothing except some declaration which would have come directly from the lips of the testatrix which would prove that there had been some undue influence, and even then the unsupported word of Hattie Irwin would hardly be sufficient. It would have required a letter, something in writing. But Hattie Irwin doesn't know Eleanor Preston. She never heard of her. She doesn't know Martha Otley. She has never heard of Martha Otley.'

'Could there have been anything else?' Brandon asked.

Selby shook his head. 'Nothing that would ensure a verdict in favour of the contestants on the ground of undue influence – nothing that I can think of.'

'It isn't a letter,' Dr Thurman said. 'I asked her if there was anything at the hotel she wanted, and asked her particularly if there were any papers or correspondence she'd brought with her. I thought perhaps – well, you know, I just wasn't taking any chances.'

'Well,' Brandon said, 'that puts us up against a brick wall.'

'If you haven't any really pertinent questions to ask her at this time,' Dr Thurman said, 'I'd much prefer to have you wait for another day or two.'

'We can't wait,' Selby said. 'The way that case is going up there, Judge Fairbanks is going to throw it out of court. We can't prove any undue influence sufficient to even get our case to the jury. At any rate, I don't think we can.'

'Well, then this witness doesn't know anything,' Dr Thurman said.

'She has to know something. Everything that Fred Albion Roff did shows that she must have known something. She must have … Wait a minute.'

Selby began pacing back and forth. Suddenly he turned, said to Dr Thurman, 'All right, Doctor, I'm ready.'

'To question her?'

'Yes.'

'Not more than two or three.'

'That's right.'

There was a gleam in Selby's eye. His manner showed suppressed excitement. 'I'm taking a gamble, Rex,' he said quietly, 'but I think it's a good gamble.'

Dr Thurman didn't waste any time. He moved over and held the door open. 'Very well, gentlemen,' he said, 'if you're ready let's go.'

They walked down the long hospital corridor. Dr Thurman gently opened the door of a private room. A nurse, standing by the bed, glanced up, smiled reassuringly at the doctor, and moved away.

Dr Thurman held the door open for Rex Brandon and Doug Selby to enter.

Hattie Irwin seemed pathetically fragile as she lay on the hospital bed, the white covers accentuating the small compass of her body. Her eyes were closed, and without the animation of those eyes, the face seemed robbed of all life, merely a work-weary mask modelled in some inanimate grey substance that had the very faintest tinge of red vitality mixed with its grey pallor. The grey hair had been combed back from the forehead and only the white pillowslip served to bring out the fact that that hair had once been dark, perhaps lustrous with the sheen of youth.

Dr Thurman stepped over to the patient, ran his hand down along her arm, raised the slender, bony wrist, placed a professional finger on the pulse. 'How are you feeling now?' he asked.

The lids slowly opened over the deep-sunken dark eyes. The woman smiled. 'Better.'

'You're doing all right,' the doctor assured her. 'Mr Selby wants to ask you just one or two questions. Don't let yourself get tired or excited. And the minute you begin to feel weary, just close your eyes. Do you understand?'

'I understand.'

Selby stepped forward. 'Mrs Irwin, were you in Olympus last fall, and did you see an automobile accident?'

For a minute, her eyes showed surprise, then she said, 'Not the accident. I was there right after the accident. They were taking out the bodies.'

'Two women?' Selby asked.

'Yes.'

'Did you see them clearly?'

'Yes. They put them on the sidewalk.'

'One of them was dead?'

'The blonde one, yes.'

'And the other?'

'I don't like to think about it. She was screaming. Then the screams died away into a gurgle. After a while they took them into a drugstore.'

Selby was silent for a moment. The eyelids of the woman on the bed fluttered.

'That's all,' Dr Thurman warned in a low voice.

Selby said, 'I think it's all right, Doctor,' and stooped to pat Hattie Irwin's shoulder reassuringly. 'I think you're going to be all right now,' he said, 'and you don't need to worry about the trip you won as your first prize. You're going to Sacramento to see your niece.'

Selby nodded to Brandon.

Dr Thurman looked puzzled as he followed them out into the corridor. 'I don't get it,' he said.

Selby smiled, 'There's one thing about Anita Eldon which isn't artificial. She's a natural blonde.'

'What does that have to do with it?' Brandon asked. 'After all, she … Oh, oh! Here comes Gifford.'

Carl Gifford came bustling into the hospital with the manner of a man who knows exactly where he is going and what he intends to do when he gets there.

'Hello,' he said, including the group in his comprehensive greeting and then, turning to Dr Thurman, said, 'I understand we have another poisoning case. Another poisoning case from the same hotel, a Hattie M Irwin this time.'

'That's right,' Brandon said.

'I want to talk with her,' Gifford announced. 'I want to find out some of the facts about that case. It may have a very direct bearing on the murder we're investigating.'

'I'm afraid you can't talk with her now,' Dr Thurman said.

'Why not?'

'She's too weak to stand another interview.'

'*Another* one!' Gifford exclaimed.

Selby said, 'Rex Brandon and I just asked her a couple of questions, Gifford.'

Gifford's face darkened. 'She only had strength for one interview, and that was given to Major Selby, a man who has no official status in this county, a man who resigned the office of district attorney and who had better keep his fingers out of …'

Rex Brandon pushed forward. 'That interview, my boy,' he said, to the angry district attorney, 'was given to me, the sheriff of this county. Any objections?'

'Lots of them,' Gifford said, his chin out, his fists clenched.

Selby pushed forward. 'Try making them to me, then.'

Gifford stared at Selby, caught the cold, purposeful glitter of Selby's eyes, said suddenly, 'All right, if you folks want to play cut-throat politics, go ahead. We'll see who wins out on *that* game.' He turned on his heel and walked off.

CHAPTER TWENTY

Selby's return to the courtroom found the contestants in a whispered conference, Judge Fairbanks plainly impatient. The last witness, who had, apparently, utterly failed to stand up under the cross-examination of A B Carr, had just left the stand and there was in Inez Stapleton's manner something of panic. Even the pompous assurance of W Barclay Stanton had been deflated to a point of almost absolute zero. He was nervously fumbling with the heavy watch chain which stretched across his big stomach.

Selby wasted no time. He had hardly entered through the swinging gate which separated the bar from the spectators' portion of the courtroom when he announced in clear, firm tones, 'Our next witness on behalf of the contestant, Barbara Honcutt, will be Helen Elizabeth Corning. Mrs Corning, will you please take the stand?'

There was a ripple of surprise throughout the courtroom. Inez Stapleton, turning hurriedly from her whispered conference, looked at Selby with an expression almost of dismay.

A B Carr's voice was suave, purring in its suggestion of triumph. 'Do I understand that *you* are calling Mrs Corning as *your* witness?'

'As our witness,' Selby said.

Carr smiled and bowed. 'Take the stand, Mrs Corning.'

While Mrs Corning was marching triumphantly to the stand, Inez Stapleton arose to crowd close to Doug Selby. 'Doug, you can't do it. She's A B's star witness, the one he's been holding in reserve. She was Martha Otley's sister. They were visiting her when Eleanor died. She'll testify to anything. I know she's prepared to smear our clients. She ...'

Selby squeezed Inez Stapleton's arm reassuringly. 'I'm playing a hunch, Inez. It *has* to be right.'

'Have you any proof?'

Selby shook his head. 'It's just a hunch.'

'I don't like it, Doug ...'

W Barclay Stanton was struggling ponderously to his feet. 'Now your Honour,' he said in the rumbling cadences which the custom of a past generation had decreed should clothe all public utterances, 'we want the record to show that this is purely and solely a responsibility of the contestant, Barbara Honcutt. The contestant, Hervey Preston, not only doesn't wish to be bound by the testimony of this witness as a witness on behalf of the contestant Hervey Preston, but upon behalf of that contestant, I protest at the legal unwisdom of calling a hostile witness at such a time and in such a manner.'

'Very well,' Judge Fairbanks said. 'Your position will be duly noted in the record, Mr Stanton. Proceed with your examination, Major Selby.'

Selby turned to size up the woman on the witness stand, a woman of about fifty-five, shrewd, crafty-eyed, firm-mouthed, a woman who was nervously smoothing down the folds of her black skirt. There was a triumphant smile lurking at the corners of her mouth, but her eyes were cautious, watchful, wary, indicating an active mind and an alert determination to make the most of the situation in which she found herself called as a witness for the contestant, who would, within certain limitations, be bound by her testimony, since she was not technically an adverse party.

A B Carr, either with a desire to educate the witness, or for the purpose of assuring the jury that Selby had placed himself in a legally impossible position, arose and said gravely to the court, 'I suggest, for the purpose of the record, your Honour, that this cannot be a move to call an adverse party under the section of the code permitting the cross-examination of such an adverse party. Helen Elizabeth Corning is the surviving sister of Martha Otley, but, inasmuch as Martha Otley dies leaving a daughter, Anita Eldon, who is her sole heir, Mrs Corning does not stand to profit one cent by the outcome of this litigation. Therefore, she cannot be deemed an adverse party, and counsel has no right to cross-examine her, but can only examine her as his own witness, and he will then be bound by her testimony.'

'Subject to the fact,' Judge Fairbanks amended, 'that within the discretion of the Court, the Court may permit leading questions of a witness who apparently is hostile in fact, regardless of whether such witness has a direct monetary interest in the outcome of the litigation.'

'Certainly, your Honour,' Carr said, smiling.

'Proceed,' Judge Fairbanks said to Selby. Selby said, 'Your name is Helen Elizabeth Corning? You live at McKeesville, Kansas, and you are the surviving sister of Martha Otley?'

'That is right.'

'You were with Martha Otley at the time of an automobile accident which occurred at Olympus, Kansas?'

'Yes.'

'And in that accident, both Eleanor Preston, the testatrix, and Martha Otley sustained injuries which proved fatal?'

'Yes.'

'Mrs Corning, can you tell us if Anita Eldon somewhat resembles her mother?'

Carr frowned perplexedly.

W Barclay Stanton started once more to lumber to his feet, apparently with an objection on his lips, then gruntingly subsided back into his chair.

'Why, yes, she has the same general resemblance, the same colour eyes, the same … She looks something like her mother looked at her age.'

'In other words, Martha Otley was a blonde. Is that right?'

'Yes.'

'And Eleanor Preston was a brunette?'

'Her hair was darker, sort of a chestnut colour.'

'And because I may be bound by the answer to this question, Mrs Corning, I want you to be very careful to confine your answer only to the question as I ask it. Mrs Corning, what was done with the injured persons immediately after that accident?'

'They were moved into a drugstore. There was a drugstore there near the corner.'

'You yourself were injured in that accident?'

'I wasn't unconscious. I had some cuts and bruises, but nothing serious.'

'And the drugstore summoned a doctor?'

'Yes. They were both dead when the doctor arrived. In fact, poor dear Eleanor had died …'

'Just a moment,' Selby interrupted, 'I'm not asking you that, since I'm going to be bound by your answers, Mrs Corning. I insist that you answer only the questions I have asked.'

'Very well,' she snapped.

'That,' Selby announced, 'is all. Do you wish to cross-examine, Mr Carr?'

'Certainly,' A B said, fully realizing the value of being able to get in the testimony of his own best witness under the guise of cross-examination.

'In that event,' Selby said, 'I think that in justice to Court and counsel, and in order to keep this witness from being charged with perjury, I now desire to state to Court and counsel, that the next witness called by the contestant, Barbara Honcutt, will be Hattie M Irwin. That Mrs Irwin is at present unable to attend court because she is under the care of a physician, but that if counsel wishes, I will *now* state to Court and counsel exactly what I expect to prove by this witness.'

'Go ahead,' Carr challenged. 'What *do* you expect to prove?'

'I expect to prove,' Selby said, 'that at the time of that automobile accident, Martha Otley died almost immediately. That Eleanor Preston lived for some few minutes until after she had been taken into the drugstore. That both were dead by the time the doctor arrived. That this witness, Helen Elizabeth Corning, acting with rare presence of mind, and realizing that in the event the beneficiary under the will died prior to the death of the testatrix, any bequests in the will to Martha Otley would be invalid, juggled the identities of the two persons and testified at the inquest that it was Eleanor Preston who died immediately and that Martha Otley survived her by a few moments. That is not true. Hattie Irwin, a witness to the accident, will swear Martha Otley was the one who died instantly, that Eleanor Preston lived for several minutes. Now then, do you wish to stipulate that Hattie M Irwin would *so* testify?'

It was to old A B Carr's credit that he showed not the faintest sign of consternation. He merely smiled and said, 'No, Major, I wouldn't wish to make any such stipulation because I am quite certain that it is entirely contrary to the facts of the case. But in view of the fact that your statement has been made in front of the jury; in view of the fact that you have boasted of your ability to produce this evidence, I am now willing to stipulate that the Court may grant a continuance until this witness of yours, Hattie M Irwin, is able to attend court. And, *then* we will see if her testimony will be as you have stated it would be and if it will stand up under cross-examination.'

And Carr's smile was a smile of conscious power, betraying no hint of inner consternation.

'I think,' Selby said to Judge Fairbanks, 'that the recess must necessarily be for more than one day.'

Judge Fairbanks frowned. 'I dislike to grant such a recess,' he said, 'after a jury has been impanelled, but, as I understand counsel's position at the present time, it is that the contestant now expects to prove that Martha Otley, the beneficiary under the will, died prior to the time Eleanor Preston met her death, and that under the law a bequest in a will to a beneficiary who is already dead is of no effect. Is that your understanding of the law, Major Selby?'

'That is my understanding of the law of this state,' Selby said, 'and I am prepared to introduce authorities to support my contention. The fact that Eleanor Preston died leaving a will, naming as her sole beneficiary, a person who was already deceased, was exactly the same, legally, as though Eleanor Preston died without leaving any will. In which event, the property must be distributed to her natural heirs – Barbara Honcutt and Hervey Preston.'

'Under the circumstances,' Judge Fairbanks said, 'the Court will take an adjournment for two days. During that time the jurors will carefully refrain from discussing this case among themselves or permitting it to be discussed in their presence, and will not form or express any opinion as to the issues involved.

'Court is adjourned.'

Doug Selby and Rex Brandon sat anxiously in Inez Stapleton's office, Inez biting at her lip in nervousness, Selby drumming incessantly on the desk. The muscles of his jaw showed how tightly he was gripping his pipe. Only Rex Brandon gave no outward sign of emotional tension.

For the fourth time in five minutes Selby looked at his watch.

'Doug,' Inez said, 'I don't see how you could have known. How you dared to take such a chance.'

'It had to be right,' Selby said. 'It's the only thing that makes sense, and we were licked the other way. It only needed one look at your faces as I entered the courtroom to know that.'

She said, 'I'll agree with you on that. The witness that was to show undue influence completely blew up under Carr's cross-examination. She just went all to pieces – couldn't be sure of anything, not even her own name.'

Selby glanced at his wristwatch again, said, 'That's the only trump card that Fred Albion Roff could possibly have had up his sleeve. It's the only thing that would have enabled him to guarantee absolutely that he could have won your case.'

'But he didn't have anything to lose if he didn't win it. He wasn't gambling anything, Doug.'

'He was gambling his time. He was gambling his expenses. He was gambling – '

The ringing of the telephone made Inez Stapleton jump as though electric wires had been affixed to the seat of her chair. She snatched up the receiver, said, 'Yes, hello. This is Inez Stapleton speaking.'

There was a moment of silence, then her face relaxed into lines of relief. She looked at Doug Selby, nodded almost imperceptibly, said, 'I understand perfectly.'

There was another period of silence, then she said, 'I'll take the matter up with my associates ... Well, that's rather short notice, you know... Well, I'll do the best I can ... All right. I'll call you back ...'

Inez Stapleton dropped the receiver into place. In a bound, she was out of the chair and rushing toward Doug Selby. Her arms circled him and she danced excitedly about his chair. 'Oh, Doug!' she exclaimed, 'you've done it!'

Rex Brandon puffed contentedly at his cigarette. 'You didn't have any doubts but what he would, did you?'

'Well, come on,' Selby said looking at his watch. 'I've got to catch a train in exactly thirty-five minutes. You're going to have to talk fast.'

'It was old A B C,' she said. 'He, of course, worked in a lot of camouflage about how his client was exceedingly nervous and wasn't standing up well under the strain of trial, and he suggests that we split the estate three ways; that Anita Eldon take a third, Barbara Honcutt take a third and Hervey Preston take a third.'

'All right,' Selby said, 'ring him up and tell him to go to hell.'

'I can't do it, Doug. I've got to take it up with W Barclay Stanton. And I hope that old stuffed-shirt isn't so anxious to grab at the bird in the hand, that he lets Carr get away with …'

'With a third of the bird in the bush,' Selby laughed. 'Don't worry. Carr would never have made that offer of compromise unless he'd taken Helen Elizabeth Corning into the privacy of his home and sweated the truth out of her. He couldn't afford to have her caught flat-footed in perjury. Now that we know the facts we can get more witnesses. If you stick it out, Carr will simply cave in and withdraw from the case. You'll never see Helen Elizabeth Corning again. Not unless Carl Gifford wants to bring her back to face a charge of perjury.'

Inez said, 'I don't know about W Barclay Stanton. He's money hungry and he may want to make some sort of a compromise. He would have sold out so cheap a couple of hours ago that almost anything will look like a godsend to him now.'

Rex Brandon said, 'If you're leaving in thirty-five minutes, Doug, let's have a little talk about that murder before you leave.'

Selby said, 'I have some ideas about that too, Rex.'

'Shoot.'

Selby said, 'Now that we know the motive for the murder, we can tell a lot more about the murder itself.'

'What do you mean?'

'Put yourself in Roff's position. He went to Los Angeles. He had information which was a two-edged sword. He could either sell it to the contestant, or he could sell it to the other side. In the one case, he caused all of the money in the estate to go in equal shares to Barbara Honcutt and Hervey Preston. In the other case, he kept quiet and it all went to Anita Eldon. He would have preferred to close with Anita Eldon because there he would be dealing with only one person. A person who was accustomed to hearing the sort of language that Fred Albion Roff wanted to use. But it was a question of who would pay the most.'

Brandon merely nodded.

Inez Stapleton, her eyes sparkling with excited animation, pushed books aside and perched on the edge of the big, flat-topped legal desk.

Almost unconsciously Selby went about the business of refilling his pipe. He pushed fresh tobacco down into the crusted bowl and lit a match before he went on.

'Now then,' he said, between the first puffs of getting the pipe going, 'you can see what happened. Roff took the matter up with Inez Stapleton, but decided not to go any farther with her because she was proving a little difficult. He turned to someone who he knew was easier.'

'Anita Eldon?'

Selby nodded.

'And Anita Eldon poisoned him?'

Selby said, 'Anita Eldon wasn't here where she could have administered the poison. And, in a case of that kind, you'd hardly put yourself in the power of someone else, by hiring a murderer to do the job for you.'

'A B Carr?' Brandon asked.

'Carr is hardly a murderer. Even though you don't agree with me about him. I somewhat doubt whether Carr knew too much about what had happened. I don't believe Carr's story about those witnesses. I do believe Carr knew two important witnesses were coming on the train, that they were to identify themselves by means of a white gardenia, and that they were to meet someone who had a white gardenia and I think Carr arranged all of the mechanics of spiriting them away. But when it came to the murder – no, Rex, there are two or three things we have to take into consideration.'

'The waiter, Henry Farley? Do you think *he's* the guilty one?'

'I don't think he could be.'

'Why not?'

'Because we must take into consideration that one of the most significant clues is that Fred Albion Roff ordered a complete breakfast just after he'd already had a breakfast.'

'Well, what does that mean?'

Selby said, 'It means that he came on to Madison City. It means that he was conducting negotiations with someone. It means that someone was in his room in the hotel and complained that he was hungry and that he hadn't had breakfast. And it means that he trapped Roff into ordering a complete breakfast sent up to his room. The minute that person heard the knock on the door which signified the waiter was bringing breakfast, that person, man or woman, stepped into the bathroom, and closed the door. Now do you get it?'

'I'm beginning to,' Brandon replied, 'but go on from there.'

'We have a murderer in the bathroom,' Selby said. 'At the very moment the waiter is putting out the breakfast things in the room, the murderer, while he is in the bathroom, is surreptitiously filling a medicine dropper with what is probably the most deadly poison commercially obtainable. The murderer waits until the waiter has left the room – then the murderer steps out of the bathroom, puts a few drops of hydrocyanic acid on each of the sugar cubes, and he's ready to proceed with the grim business in hand.'

'But the coffee was part of the breakfast,' Brandon pointed out.

Selby nodded. 'The murderer must have said, "I don't drink coffee," and suggested to Roff that perhaps another cup of coffee would be acceptable to him even if he had had breakfast. It would keep the coffee from going to waste.'

Brandon's eyes narrowed. 'You're giving a pretty good theory there, Doug.'

'And,' Selby said, 'the murderer simply stalled around until Roff fell for the bait of a cup of steaming hot coffee. Remember Roff was trying to put across a delicate business deal – one which involved blackmail, the suppression of evidence and the subornation of perjury. That's why Roff would have been better off to have sold out to the contestants. If he'd done that, he could then have kept himself in a purely ethical position of merely producing a witness to testify to one bomb-shell fact that would blast Anita Eldon's case completely out of court. When he started dealing with Anita Eldon, he had to adopt the position of suppressing evidence and tacitly consenting to the commission of perjury. Roff was a lawyer, and he didn't want to do that, but he was greedy and when it came to a showdown he did it. But he was nervous. That extra cup of coffee tempted him. And killed him.'

'And the murderer?' Brandon asked.

Selby said, 'The murderer then proceeded to clean out all the papers from Roff's briefcase.'

'Why didn't he take the briefcase?'

'Because then, when the body was identified, the missing briefcase would have proven that Roff had been killed because someone was afraid of certain papers he had in his briefcase, and that would have, in itself, been a clue. So the murderer left only the new pad of legal foolscap that Roff had purchased and which was already in the briefcase.'

'Go ahead,' Brandon said. 'He took the papers, then what?'

'Then,' Selby said, 'he didn't want to leave the room simply carrying a lot of loose papers. That in itself might attract suspicion. He couldn't be absolutely certain that when he stepped out in the corridor he wouldn't meet someone. Roff had already opened his bag and taken out the soiled shirts and underwear. The murderer rolled them into a bundle as though making up a bundle of laundry, and he put the papers on the inside of the bundle.'

'And then?' Brandon asked.

'Of course,' Selby said, 'I'm just reasoning from step to step, Rex, putting myself in the position of the murderer and ...'

'Go ahead, son,' Rex Brandon interrupted.

'Well,' Selby went on, 'he went out into the corridor, and he took the bundle down to his own room and he disposed of the clothes. We don't know yet just how he disposed of them, but he disposed of them quickly and very effectively. And then, he started checking over the papers, and he found that one page was missing from a brief. Had he dropped that page in the corridor, or had he left it in the briefcase, or had it been dropped somewhere on the floor of the room?'

'So the murderer walked back down the corridor and didn't see the single sheet of paper that was missing. So he knew someone had found it. And he probably telephoned A B Carr a tip that two witnesses, who were vitally important in that will contest case, were coming to Madison City and that Carr should pick them up. And he ... wait a minute, Rex. He'd fixed that up before. The murder had been deliberately planned, and he'd arranged with Anita Eldon to wear a white gardenia so that Carr could identify her. That would give Carr an out in case …'

'You don't think Anita Eldon arranged it all herself?' Brandon asked.

'She couldn't,' Selby said, hurriedly looking at his watch. 'She wasn't there. It had to be someone who was in the hotel, someone who could move back and forth.'

'A woman,' Brandon said, 'because of Coleman Dexter's testimony.'

'Not a woman,' Selby said. 'Remember that the murderer wanted to account for the presence of the paper in the corridor, and at the same time he wanted to blame the crime on someone else and divert suspicion from himself. Why not testify that he had seen a woman, whom he described somewhat vaguely, leaving the room with a bundle of laundry and dropping a paper. That would put him in the clear … Rex, I've got to sprint to get packed up and get to my train. I simply have to make that train. You check up on Coleman Dexter. Remember that Anita Eldon must have had some business manager with whom she suggested Fred Albion Roff communicate, someone who was empowered to act. Probably someone who lived at the Madison Hotel, since Roff hadn't had any outside visitors to his room from the time he arrived until the time he was murdered. Get Dexter, Rex, and check up on him.'

Selby tapped the ashes out of his pipe, looked at it longingly for a moment, then suddenly thrust the warm bowl into Rex Brandon's hand. 'I won't take this with me, Rex. Put it back in the office desk and leave it until I get back from wherever I'm going.'

Brandon thrust the pipe into his pocket, enveloped Doug Selby's hand into his own. 'It's a good theory, Doug. At least it's worth a try. You've got the mechanics of the murder worked out all right. I'm not so certain about Dexter.'

199

'Give him a once-over,' Selby said. 'But that's the way the thing must have happened, and he could have easily moved over to Hattie Irwin's table and planted the arsenic.'

'And planted the bottle of hydrocyanic acid and the medicine dropper in Farley's room?'

'Sure,' Selby said. 'That was the obvious thing for him to do.'

'And old A B Carr?'

Selby shook his head and smiled. 'You'll never catch him. His trail is covered too well.'

'You mean he got this man, Floris, who was shepherding Mrs Irwin around, to show up and ...'

'No, no,' Selby said hurriedly. 'Floris may have been working for the murderer. You *might* even tie him up to Carr – if you can ever find him, but I doubt it. Perhaps Anita Eldon engaged Floris. They had to work fast and they either didn't have time to get him to the train or they deliberately used Carr to break the trail. Old A B Carr probably didn't know there'd been a murder committed, but he did know that a plot was on foot to suppress some evidence. Carr was willing to take a certain part in it, but he wasn't going to go far enough to get his fingers burned. While he was meeting the witnesses at the train, the man who was scheduled to get the woman out of the country ... Rex, I really haven't any more time. I've got to sprint.'

Inez Stapleton slid down off the desk.

'You have time for one more thing.'

'What?'

'My thanks,' she said, and her arms were suddenly around his neck, her warm lips on his.

Rex Brandon pulled the big silver turnip timepiece out of his pocket, looked at it, scratched his head, thrust it back. 'You got three minutes, son,' he said, and walked out of the office, his eyes deliberately fixed straight ahead.

CHAPTER TWENTY-ONE

Sylvia Martin was at the train as Selby leapt out of the taxicab and dashed across the station platform.

Her eyes were laughing up into his. 'Thought you weren't going to make it, Doug. I even hoped you wouldn't.'

'I had to, Sylvia.'

'How's it coming, Doug?'

'I don't know,' Selby said. 'Get in touch with Rex Brandon for the story and wire me aboard the train. Rex has the number of my reservations.'

'All aboard!' the conductor yelled.

Sylvia clung to his arm. 'Doug, it was so good – so darn good – Doug, come back. Promise me you'll come back?'

Selby bent to kiss her, was unconscious of slamming vestibule doors, of the clanging of the bell. The long train slowly creaked into motion.

It was Sylvia who suddenly pushed him away, laughing. 'Get on that train, idiot. You can't stand here kissing me all day. Hurry!'

The porter of the last car was grinning, running alongside the car, holding the vestibule door open.

Selby sprinted, swung aboard, the porter after him. Selby turned to wave wildly at Sylvia Martin, saw her smiling face until she suddenly turned away, undoubtedly to hide a sudden rush of tears.

The porter was grinning at Selby's mouth and Selby, somewhat self-consciously, took out his handkerchief and wiped off the lipstick as he entered the roomette which had been reserved for him.

Sitting at the train window, he watched the familiar sights of Madison City gliding slowly by. The white courthouse up on the hill, the exclusive residential district. He could even pick out the big white stucco house in which Alfonse Baker Carr had signified his wish to live while he retired from active practice.

It seemed to Selby as though he were leaving behind him much that was unfinished, a segment of his life that must someday be resumed. But ahead of him lay something vastly more important; something that must be accomplished if Madison City were to remain as it had been.

The train gathered speed. The whistle boomed out its signal for a grade crossing.

Selby moistened his lips and some of the flavour of Sylvia Martin's lipstick still clung to them. Almost automatically he reached for his handkerchief, and then stayed his hand; his head rested back against the cushion and he closed his eyes.

It was at San Luis Obispo that he received Rex Brandon's wire:

MAJOR DOUGLAS SELBY
ROOMETTE 6 CAR 41
YOUR HUNCH CORRECT DEXTER PROVEN TO HAVE BEEN SECRETLY MARRIED ANITA ELDON REFUSES CONFESS AND HAS RETAINED CARR AS LAWYER BUT HIS FINGERPRINTS FOUND ON INSIDE BATHROOM DOOR AND FRAGMENTS OF CHARRED PAPER IDENTIFIED AS FROM ROFF'S BRIEFCASE FOUND IN HIS ROOM CONGRATULATIONS PROBABLY CAN'T STICK CARR WITH ANYTHING BUT HAVE HIM WORRIED AND DOING LOT OF EXPLAINING GIFFORD ALSO

EXPLAINING HAVE YOUR PIPE IN MY DESK DRAWER
WAITING FOR YOU TO COME BACK CLEAN UP ON THE
JAPS YOURS FOR KEEPS

REX BRANDON

ERLE STANLEY GARDNER

THE CASE OF THE CARELESS CUPID

Selma Arlington is engaged to a wealthy widower. His heirs don't want him to tie the knot. Perry Mason is asked by Selma to prove she is neither a gold-digger nor a murderer of her first husband, but incriminating evidence comes to light.

THE CASE OF THE FENCED-IN WOMAN

Morley Eden finds an unwanted guest on his property. The ex-wife of his dream house's contractor claims that the property is one-half hers. Eden calls upon Perry Mason to resolve a dispute that is linked to murder.

ERLE STANLEY GARDNER

THE CASE OF THE MISCHIEVOUS DOLL

A mysterious young woman, Dorrie Ambler, wishes to prove her identity to Perry Mason. She wants him to witness her appendectomy scar, claiming she has a double. The double turns out to be Minerva Minden, madcap heiress of Montrose. Mason has his work cut out for him when his investigation leads him to a dead man in an apartment building.

THE CASE OF THE PHANTOM FORTUNE

Horace Warren pays five hundred dollars to have Perry Mason attend a buffet dinner to observe his guests. He also wants Mason to investigate a fingerprint and suspects his wife is being blackmailed. Mrs Warren's mystery past may hold the clues.

ERLE STANLEY GARDNER

THE CASE OF THE POSTPONED MURDER

Perry Mason is hired to protect Mae Farr from a presumed stalker, wealthy playboy Penn Wentworth. When Mason learns that Wentworth wants Mae for forging his name on a cheque, things get complicated. But fatal gunplay leaves Wentworth dead, Mae a wanted woman and Perry Mason in trouble.

THE CASE OF THE RESTLESS REDHEAD

Evelyn Bagby has ambition, bad luck – and red hair. When she is caught with stolen diamonds it looks like an airtight case. But Perry Mason believes she has been set up. Then comes news of another crime and Mason finds the charge against his client is murder.